FIELDING DAWSON

WILL SHE UNDERSTAND?

NEW SHORT STORIES

COLLAGES BY THE AUTHOR

SANTA ROSA

BLACK SPARROW PRESS

1988

Many of these appeared in the following publications: *Issue #1 & 2, Multiples, Writing, S.C.A.T., Ninth Decade, Exquisite Corpse, Bread, North Atlantic Review, 2nd & 3rd Blind Date, Red Weather, Witness.*

The fan letter on page 45 is from Eliot Greenspan, and is used with his permission.

LIBRARY OF CONGRESS CATALOGING-IN-PUBLICATION DATA

Dawson, Fielding, 1930–
    Will she understand? : new short stories / Fielding Dawson : collages by the author.
        p.   cm.
ISBN   0-87685-730-6:   ISBN 0-87685-729-2 (pbk.) :
ISBN 0-87685-731-4 (signed) :
    I. Title.
PS3554.A948W5   1988
813'.54 – dc19   88-2450
                              CIP

In Memory of Frances Byars

"That's the trick of mortality: baby, you will live until the end, and there is no end."

—William Saroyan
The Comic Page and Vital Statistics

CONTENTS

Will She Understand?
New Short Stories

Singing Stars and Stripes Forever

A CHINESE MAN with an axe in his right hand walked out the front door of the restaurant he owned, turned the corner, and chopped down a thirty foot ginkgo tree.

A neighborhood committee had planted it, as they had others, along the avenue, and on certain side streets. Four hundred dollars each. Causing a little war, a boycott of that restaurant, and reintroducing a bygone racism: the Yellow Peril had come to town. They were serious, and, were here to stay.

Passers-by were shocked at the small stump in that small square of dirt. The big metropolitan papers, however, considered it insignificant, so no one knew what had happened until, on the front page of a giveaway neighborhood paper a lady reporter broke the news, naming the restaurant owner's name, and that of his restaurant, including his motive, as well as the history of the ginkgo.

LAND OF WOK OWNER CHOPS DOWN TREE

A brief, but detailed report.

The Story:

Business had been good, and as he had done with his other restaurant, across town, he wanted to extend out onto the sidewalk an enclosed cafe. Applied to the city for permission, permission granted. He chopped down the ginkgo, it was in his way. But the day the news broke, business went downhill so fast any fool foresaw disaster, and those persons not from the neighborhood, choosing to eat in LAND OF WOK, perchance, were puzzled and perhaps hurt at the cold, and angry glares they received from people passing by. So, the owner, giving it his last shot, appeared before a district citizens group who had blocked his sidewalk cafe plan. They heard his plea in excellent English, and his promise to plant a new ginkgo, which he did. But he gave up his idea, and sold out to newcomers, who, eager to open up in America, soon became baffled, sad and bitter, for no one would eat in the new HUNAN DREAM, ever, except strangers to the neighborhood.

Everyone thought the former owner had retreated to his other

11

restaurant, across town, to lick his wounds, and make fresh plans, but he did nothing of the kind. He bought out a Ukrainian shoemaker and dry cleaning establishment two blocks north of HUNAN DREAM, renovated it, and opened up a restaurant with a new name, not using the word WOK.

Business is good. There are two ginkgos in front, having been planted by the neighborhood committee before the Ukrainians opened up. All who boycotted LAND OF WOK before and HUNAN DREAM at present, enjoy his cooking no end.

The Ukrainian shoemaker and dry cleaning family moved to a new location a few blocks south, and with the money WOK paid them, opened up again. He paid 'em a *lot,* clever and ambitious man, but not stingy. Their business is good, too.

The Reason

ONE LATE EVENING in the fall of 1957, a young, small, slender fair-skinned lad with a powdered white wig and big ears was walking through Sheridan Square, in Greenwich Village.

He turned left, crossed through a park with low iron railings and dark figures on benches.

His destination appeared before him.

The Cafe Bohemia.

The front door was open, music flowed out, and swirled in the air.

The small fellow walked in and along the almost deserted bar, and took a seat near the darkened service area. He ordered a glass of white wine. Got it. Paid. Sipped. Glanced at shadowed couples seated at a few tables in front of the bandstand, or stage. He focused his attention on a small, slender, young black man in dark glasses. Dark jacket raglan sleeves. Stovepipe pants. His right hand held a twinkling golden trumpet at his side as he stood, center stage, between two overhead red spots, in the dark, snapping his fingers, and nodding his head. The man with the trumpet was Miles Davis, and he was listening to a tenor saxophone solo by John Coltrane, who stood to his left. Just beyond John, Philly Joe Jones played drums, and on his left, Paul Chambers on bass.

The piano was behind Miles, to his left, Red Garland at the keyboard.

The gentleman sitting at the bar, sipping white wine and watching, or seeming to watch, for in truth he was listening with an attentive and disciplined ear, and an interest to match that of the man on stage with the trumpet. The little man at the bar may have looked odd, with his funny powdered hair, and big ears, but a closer look at his expression told a far different story: his face was of complete quietude, as in the concentration toward composing: he was hearing the music as if it were written. Oh no one would dare say it. Never. The men up on stage were the very stars of spontaneity . . .

Miles Davis noticed him.

And on the break, as John, Philly Joe, Red and Paul walked outside for a smoke, the gentleman at the bar spoke —

"Miles," he said. Miles stopped. Looked through dark glasses at the other man, feeling a sense they had met, but couldn't place where.

"Yeah," Miles whispered. Voice raspy. "Have we met?"

The other smiled. "Not in fact," he said. "But we have something in common."

"We do?"

"Yes. Music."

Miles frowned, gave the fellow a pointed look, parted his lips — "I don't believe it."

The young man with big ears was amused. Turned — "Excuse me, bartender? Could I have a pencil and a piece of paper?"

The bartender found pencil and paper, slid them across to the youth who said,

"Look at this," to Miles.

Miles leaned close, and watched the other man write with incredible swiftness — left to right, new lines, left to right, left to right, zip zip zip, what Miles had just played. Miles asked,

"How do you know that?"

The other fellow gave a merry little laugh, and his eyes twinkled, and as in a dream, leaving Miles perplexed, perhaps, the scene changed, quick and easy as a happy fancy, or a puzzle, like listening to A Little Night Music, *It Never Entered My Mind*. They sounded the same.

Mary Will Be Good for Warren

—for Rudy

AT A PARTY in the suburbs. Isobelle, nicknamed Belle, played the kitchen radio, looking for some decent rock. On her third gin martini, her language was lucid. Hostess amused. Belle's husband not.

He helped himself to two slices of turkey, with hot dressing, hot gravy, peas, mashed potatoes and cranberry jelly. Napkin, silverware. Cold bottle of Eagle beer.

Went into the den where he sat in a chair beside a coffee table on which he placed his meal, switched on a white tensor lamp, and pushed the remote control button on the arm of the chair. *Casablanca* sprang into perfect focus on the 24″ screen of the set that was part of a bookcase across the room. The farewell scene in Paris, filmed in classic, medium two-shots, cut to closeup, music, theme rising, cut to commercial.

He forked turkey, peas and mashed potatoes into his mouth, as a beautiful young blonde woman appeared on screen, treading water near the edge of a pool. She smiled, gave him a sidelong look, and said,

"Hey, I want to talk to you."

Climbed out of the pool, picked up a blue towel, draped it over her shoulders, like a cape, and gathered it around her front as he glanced at the fork of cranberry jelly, aware of someone beside him, and took a look, as she had, or, rather, smiled down to him as he was looking up, she said hi, pulled a chair over and sat down.

"I read one of your books," she said. "I don't think it would be good for a movie, but you sure are good." She leaned across, helped herself to a bite of turkey and sip of Eagle. She smelled great. "Would you dry my back?"

As he dried her back—she was thin, but her skin creamy smooth, and soft, she had a roundness he, like fifty million other guys, found appealing. He held out the towel. She stood up, took it, and with a glance of mock reproach, dried her legs, very, very elegant.

"The book about the mountain."

"Oh yes," he said. "But it's wrong for you."

She folded the towel, put it on the floor between them, sat down, and looked at the towel, and as following a bird into flight, her dark blue eyes rose until they met his. Her lips parted: "I need a writer."

15

He laughed, about to ask—Why me?

"I want someone different." She paused, and said, "What I mean is," beginning a slow, no joke breathtaking grin, eyes twinkling in self-amusement (on camera): "Do you have something for *me*?" Her eyes were creased at the edges, and hard in the centers, sensual pink lips a thin line in a ghost of a smile. It gave him the jitters.

He thought of the two feature-length scripts that had gone the circuit, received high praise, in boxes on a shelf.

"Maybe," he said.

"You have something?" She put her hand on his wrist. Hot hand. She took it away.

"Maybe," he repeated. His scalp prickled.

She rose, crossed to a desk, found a pad of blank paper and a ball point pen. Scribbled, handed it to him.

"This is my telephone number. Call me tomorrow morning, we'll make a date to get together, okay?"

"Okay."

"Excuse me," she smiled, warm, sincere. "I have to go back to work."

He reached down, picked up the towel, gave it to her as he rose from his chair, to shake her hand, but she shook her head, told him to close his eyes, which he did, and hearing her laughter, opened them. She was swimming away from the camera, across the pool, in full color. She turned, cut to classic tv medium shot, waved her hand, big grin, and called:

"It was fun meeting you!" Cut to closeup. "*Don't* forget to call this number!" An AT&T ad. The number appeared on screen, as an amused male voice, off screen, read off the digits. He glanced at the slip of paper. Different number.

The next day he called, and they got together in a coffee shop in the Village. He gave her both scripts (had half dozen extra copies, just in case), telling her which one he thought best for her. And, no hurry. He stressed she not rush through, read them with care, he'd hope for the best.

A few weeks later she phoned him. They met in the same place, and knowing by the feel of these things that she wasn't interested, he wondered how she would break the bad news. And was disappointed to hear the line he'd heard so often. But she was being nice about it, and though she made him nervous—magnetic beauty always before the camera—it was fun being in the illusion that she needed him.

Over lime sherbert.

"I like them, very much." Thoughtful. Serious expression became wistful. "I read them. I enjoyed them." Candid, direct. "But," she

16

sighed, gestured. "Neither is quite right, for me."

He wondered if he should be direct, in turn. Sure.

"You know why, don't you?"

Watching his words place the responsibility of comprehension on her pretty shoulders. She had a nice tan, smooth and brown all over, large round white-rimmed dark glasses, curly blonde hair peeping out under the New York Yankee ballcap her boyfriend had gotten her. Red plastic sandals from Paris, a nifty yellow cotton jumper, blue buttons.

As she fought not to gape, she gaped, trying to keep her eyes sly, they popped wide open, as she fought even harder not to stutter and stammer, she managed to ask,

"What do you mean?"

"I mean, as they stand, they are not for you. I told you, they *might* be — I said *maybe*. Okay, they aren't. But in a rewrite, the part most suited for you is that of Mil, Peggy's sister. Peggy marries Howard. The way I think of it, I'd remove Peggy, and have Mil — you — take her place, so that Mil marries Howard, and with a little work, make her the star figure.

He smiled.

She didn't.

Her eyes had rolled over and were searching through her memory.

"*Lazy Green Dog,*" he said. The title of the script. She nodded, as in a dream.

"Howard meets Peggy in the airline terminal, Lambert Field, in St. Louis. He bumps into her. She's with her sister, Mil."

Her face was slack, without expression, in the intensity of it, searching searching, in her brain, echo chambers: *Lambert Lambert, St. Louis Louis Louis, Peggy Peggy Peggy, Howard Howard Howard, Mil Mil Mil,* click. End.

She looked at him.

"Slice of life story."

He'd broken his heart on that script.

"You can write anything," she said, by way of apology. She grinned that grin millions had witnessed. Say! Could she read some of his short stories, maybe find an idea for a feature?

Why not?

They set it up. He'd had two books of stories published, and had extra copies. So he called her the day he said he would but her boyfriend said she'd gone to L.A.

His wife, Belle, over coffee after breakfast, the next day, said, "Out to Hollywood, huh?" Pause. "She say when she'll be back?"

"No."

"Why?"

"She doesn't know. Cut it out." Pause. "Something will happen."

That night, at supper:

"Did she say what will happen? No! She *can't*! Neither can you! You know those people! They even *lie* in generalizations!" Pause. "Did you give her your books?"

"No," he said. "Not yet."

"How many will you?"

"Two. The short stories."

"There's forty bucks down the drain," she sneered. "Plus tax."

"Less tax," he replied. "But how else am I to know? She might like one! Fuck the tax. I can't call her a liar, she gave me good advice." She had said if he wanted to write for television he had to watch it. An agent had once told him if he wanted to write for the slick magazines, he had to read them. But he hated tv and despised the slicks. So. "I have to follow through. I'd be a fool not to."

"Unh huh." She made a face. "But *I* don't, and *I* live with *you,* and you're an asshole. She's not that beautiful."

"That's irrational."

"I don't care."

Several weeks later, the actress called, back in town from the west coast, sounding weary. Said she wanted to rest. She'd call him in a week or so. She hadn't forgotten.

She called, and he invited her over. His wife and her friend Maggie went to an afternoon movie. "Good luck," she had said.

And seeing the beautiful youthful movie star face and figure walk up the stairs after watching Belle go down them was indeed a contrast.

But beauty was forlorn.

She'd made some mistakes. Four years ago, things had looked great, but after the tv series (in which she co-starred in a cowboy/cowgirl/western-style detective team) was cancelled, and the parts in her first three movies — while good — didn't lead to bigger and better parts, it all seemed hopeless. And going for big parts or nothing, she rejected offers until, to her surprise, the offers stopped. Her agent was helpless. So she returned to New York with her boyfriend, did some soul searching, was back on her feet again, and it'd be great if he could write something for her.

He made some coffee. They talked, seated at the table in the rear, by the fire escape. Nice, warm day out.

"Do you still see Warren?" he asked.

"Sure," she said, in a reflective way. "We're friends." He wondered if he might say something so she would talk about herself, although

18

he knew nothing of her world. He said he thought *Shampoo* was a little too long, but a good movie. She agreed, a cloud crossed her face on the mention of Goldie, for it seemed she should have had Goldie's part. Not knowing what to say, he said,

"I thought it was an honest movie for Warren, hairdresser and all, I thought he was honest."

"Oh yes," she gestured, it was true, "all those girls, that's the way he is. He can't help it, just like he said." She murmured: "Mary will be good for him. But —" pause — "he lives in that castle out there. It's so big, and dark. No paintings, or anything, and it's so *cold.* I've been there. He has a theater in his basement, and he watches movies, you know . . ." she made a vague smile, but looked helpless, "with the girls. And they keep on coming!"

They smiled because the pun wasn't funny. He gave her his two books of short stories, indicating the ones he'd marked in red on the table of contents. He stood beside her, finger on each title, hoping she'd remember. She thanked him, put the books in her bag, bag on the table.

They talked about books.

He had just read *Congo,* and thought the end was a —

"Cop out," she interrupted. "I read it, too. I know Michael."

"You do?"

"Sure. We're friends. I'm in his new movie."

He felt his face redden, at a loss for words.

"May I use your phone?"

"Yes," he said, rejecting the wisecrack hoping she wouldn't call Warren, and watched her cross the room, lift the receiver and dial. "I'm calling my agent," she said over her shoulder. Gazed out the window beyond the fire escape, at houses across the street, and he had a funny feeling she was in a movie.

"Hi," she said. The way she stood. As if he wasn't there but she wanted him there, so he was there. She identified herself. Waited. He heard a faint voice. She nodded, murmuring, yes, okay, well, I don't know. "Do you think I'm right for it?"

Faint voice.

"No," she smiled. "It isn't me." Pause. "Yes. Tomorrow. Bye." Hung up, turned to face the writer across the room (two over-the-shoulder P.O.V. long shots), and (long shot from the fire escape) walked toward him, speaking —

"What do *you* think? He wanted me for a linen commercial. Sheets! *Me!* Do you think I'd look good under a sheet? I don't have any tits!" She laughed, hard. "How can a girl with no tits do a linen commercial?"

He, embarrassed, was silent.

"Well," she said. "I have to go to the beauty parlour." Fluffed her hair, put on her jacket, picked up her bag. "I'm a mess." She does need a writer, he thought, and walked with her to the front door.

"You're beautiful and you know it."

She smiled, demure.

He opened the door, she stepped into the hall, turned—

"Jack's in town. Did you know?"

"No."

"Yes," she said. "For his new movie—*Postman*."

"Ah yes."

"There's a party tonight, and I want to see him. I love Jack."

The writer's head spun.

"I was at a party with Warren," she continued, "and, you know how he stands there, and waits for the girls to come to him—"

"Which they do."

"Yes, and I was so bored I walked around, and saw Jack with some of his friends. I'd never met him, so I went over and—"

Raised her head with a stiff upper lip:

"I said, '*I love you.*'"

Wow. "What did he do?"

"We left. His friends are wonderful. Jack's a great talker. Tells terrific stories. Warren listens."

"Is Warren jealous?"

"Maybe. But they're very good friends, you know. There's nothing—"

"No. Of course not."

Pause.

She put a hand on her bag, letting him know she wouldn't forget. Smiled, took a step toward him. He to her. They kissed. A peck.

He almost blushed he felt so silly, what an odd script! yet he allowed the illusion to prevail, and said,

"I'll call Friday morning, eleven."

"Swell," she said, then paused. "All we need is money."

"I'll write anything you want."

Her face softened. "Don't worry," and the camera was on her. She was radiant. Close up. "Something will happen."

"Great."

"Bye!"

And she was gone.

He called on Friday at eleven, her boyfriend said she was in L.A. Had left yesterday afternoon. Be back on Monday.

Had she read the books?

Books? He couldn't say . . .

20

Her boyfriend was an artist. The two guys knew each other. They talked about their work a little, some about baseball and said take care.

Isn't that funny, he said to himself. What should I do? I can't just wait.

Think.

So he thought. And thought. What to do?

But who would know?

Doctor Wurlie!

Of course!

Old pal and screen writer!

He dialed. Waited.

"I'm not at home," the tape of the Doctor's voice said, and after the recorded message and famous tone, the writer followed taped instructions: identified himself, gave the day and date, said he needed advice on a possible screenwriting job. "Give me a call, would you?" And gave his telephone number. "Thanks."

That afternoon the good Wurlie called. The writer told him about the actress. In brief.

"When is she coming back?"

"Monday."

"Listen, I'm in a pay phone in Toronto. I'll be back Monday night. Call her on Monday, and call me on Tuesday and let me know what she says. Okay?"

"Great."

He called her Monday morning.

"Hi!" she said. He, astonished she was there. "I'm very sorry," she said, "but I got a call from L.A. and I had to go. You know."

"I know," he said. The books. The books. The books.

"I'm a third of the way into the first one, the one you said I should read first." Pause. "I love it."

He smiled.

"Could you call me Thursday?" Pause. "Morning?"

Fine.

Next day he phoned the Doctor, who told him to call him after he spoke with her on Thursay, which he did. Called her Thursday morning. She was in L.A. Had she landed something? Her boyfriend said yes. He phoned Doctor Wurlie.

"I thought so," he said. "These people are invisible." Pause. "Who is she? I mean, has she been in any movies?"

"Did you see *Cry Baby?*"

"No, but I know who wrote it. It wasn't very good."

"No. But she knows people."

He told him. Warren, Mary, Jack, Goldie, Michael.

"The director."

"The novelist."

They laughed.

"I know Michael," Wurlie said. "I heard you have a new novel out. Is that right?"

"Yes."

Gave brief details. Publisher, his editor, book length, and storyline.

"Sounds good. Can I read it?"

"Sure. Want to get together?"

They did. In Wurlie's kitchen, at a small table by a window with hanging plants, flowers. View of back yards. He had brought a copy of his novel, which he inscribed for him. They drank herbal tea and talked. Wurlie talked about the decade he'd spent, curing sick screenplays "around the pool." Rose from the table, crossed the room to a shelf below cabinets, went through a pile of color postcards until he came to one, of a skeleton, stretched out, in pieces, in sand, amid cacti. Beside its hip, a canteen. Wurlie gave his friend a knowing look. Said,

"The celluloid trail."

He read his friend's novel. Phoned to thank him, say how much he liked it. Wished him all success.

"At last!" his wife exclaimed. "Somebody real! I like him! I'd even like to meet him!"

Again, the Doctor called.

"Tell me once again," he said. "Who is this chick?"

The writer explained, in reasonable detail.

"Never heard of her," Wurlie said.

"Do you want me to phone Michael?"

The writer didn't know what to say.

"I don't know what to say," he said.

"Listen," Wurlie said. "Forget her. She needed a project, and from what you say, she's got one." He paused. "I don't mean to disappoint you, but she might never finish your books."

The writer was disappointed.

"They're like that," Wurlie continued. "Get excited on one thing, make all kinds of promises and then forget it. If we have an idea, we develop a treatment, and go to producers and directors. Not actors." He paused. "Or actresses."

"Good advice." Pause. "She knows Jack."

"So do I. Want me to phone him?"

A writer amazed.

"Do you want to?"

"No, but I could. Look, do you want to know what she's up to?"

"Do you think it matters?"

"No, but—it's strange I don't know her."

"She was at the party for him. Here. He came to town for—"

"*The Postman* movie. I know. I was at that party. What does she look like?"

The other, no longer able to contain himself, laughed until Wurlie, himself, laughed. What happened next didn't matter, because everything fell through, directors and producers notwithstanding. And somewhere along the way, the writer and his wife were in a restaurant downtown, and they ran into the actress and her boyfriend. Embraces, kisses. Standing at the bar, drinks in hand, exciting to hear about her new movie. She had a good part, it would be out soon. The news of who else was starring in it caused ahhhs and oh mys, all fun, in that illusion.

"I didn't finish your books," she admitted. "But I will!"

Happy.

The writer nodded. His wife smiled, and said, out of the corner of her mouth: "Wurlie sure called *that* shot."

Before they parted, the actress said, in a tone of voice far different than her camera smile, and fleeting serious glance, to let him know:

"I won't forget you."

The writer nodded.

"Nor shall I forget you," he smiled.

And in sparkle, good night, good night, each of the four people, although the central two in particular, knew what that meant. "I won't forget you" was the rest of your life, in the movie business. Just in case.

The Song

SHE WAS A SMALL, short woman with a round face, pug nose, bright brown eyes and gray hair piled and pinned all around her head.

His Aunty Mary.

His grandfather had been a poet, and Aunty Mary, being a musician, put Papa's poems to music, and on many an evening, in all seasons, his Aunty Dot sang, while Mary played. Papa's songs.

Broadway show tunes, too, and songs from the First War, the 20s, 30s, sheet music, a couple of French favorites, a lot of English songs, with selections from Gilbert and Sullivan, and from the large hardcover book with illustrations, *American Favorites,* always up there, above the keyboard. Ready for action. In particular the section of Stephen Foster, within which, a favorite which she sang and played with zip, zest and laughter: *The Camptown Races,* although everybody knew *Mandalay* was, hands down, the boy's special favorite, but in a different way, he felt at home with a funny little song called *Billy Boy.*

And as the Second World War ground its way to its unthinkable end, and the decade progressed to war clouds over Korea, he went away to college, leaving home and maybe the world behind him, in the spirit of his treasured book of childhood: *My Name is Aram,* he leapfrogged the rim of where he had been, onto the edge of where he would go, from whence, with true Saroyan nerve, he somersaulted into his future.

Didn't know how much of Saroyan he'd taken until it began to appear in his vocabulary, and letters, which ceased in his second year in college. He began reading Faulkner and Joyce.

As a small, bright star too far away to be recognized but sparkling enough to be seen, wherever the young man went, *Billy Boy* followed, way back there behind his ears, along with other stars, but unlike any, *Oh where have you been Billy Boy, Billy Boy, Oh where have you been, charming Billy?*

They had laughed, often near tears, as they sat on the piano bench, her hands in her lap, his in his, it was so crazy, their song of reflection, for they were in each other's eyes: Where had he been? meant where was he going? To look for the joy of his life, in 1944, aunts and uncles on the front porch, morning glories, honeysuckle, red roses, green lawns, iced tea, but he's a young thing, and cannot leave his mother. Aunty Mary was an unmarried virgin, but in the song, she'd be his mother, he was fourteen, she at least sixty, and they sang no other words of the lyric but those, in the song. Their song.

The Blue in the Sky

On Friday, August 30th, 1985, the drummer Philly Joe Jones died, in Philadelphia. He was 62. He became known while playing with the Miles Davis Quintet in the late 50s, and called himself Philly Joe to make it clear he wasn't Jo Jones, although if you listened it was already clear. He hit hard, in contrasts: bass drum, gut tom-tom, crossfire of sticks on cymbals.

Four days later, on Tuesday, September 3rd, 1985, Jo Jones died. He was 73, and lived in Manhattan. He played drums for Count Basie from 1935 until 1948 when he cut out on his own, to become a legend. Nat Hentoff writes in the *Voice* that Jo Jones played like the wind, and quoted Max Roach, who said:

"For every three beats a drummer plays, he owes Jo five."

ON A COLD NIGHT in late January, 1954, a young man who had just finished basic training, was home on leave, before sailing to Germany where he would complete his tour of duty.

He was with two friends, Gene and Gary, and they were on their way, in Gene's car, to East St. Louis, Sin City itself, right across the Mississippi, to hear some music.

East St. Louis in those days was counterpart to Chicago's Calumet City. There wasn't a lot of glamor, but there was some, and there were whores and gangsters, crooked police and all kinds of creeps: dangerous, very dangerous, drunk, not so drunk, the bored and eager businessmen, even a few innocents, a few, and, ever death to good music and happy saloons: college kids with money.

But there was music, and the whole city was against the law. From the big nightclubs, the glittering, hard-drinking, gambling, dancing and fun palaces at the foot of the bridge, to the heart of the Strip. Restaurants, hotdog and hamburger joints, bars, penny arcades, jukebox dancehalls, casinos, strip joints, and bars, more restaurants, casinos and strip joints, following the river to a rundown roadhouse beyond, crouched in darkness near a junkyard: a one-storey, shabby and forbidding place with no name, or cause, save college throats, down which flowed beer and peanuts, chips, french fries and ketchup and onions and hamburgers, up which they often returned — fast, vomit covered the floors of bathrooms, where in a horror of smells, as the young man — in heart a poet — myself — took a piss on many a night, I looked out an open, woodframed window, into darkness, at scattered lights across the Mississippi, reflected twinkling, on the midnight water.

Gene found a parking place near the beginning of the strip. A few yards down from a blue glass front door of a white stucco nightclub with a red and white striped awning and a placard outside, advertising Charlie Barnett and his orchestra. Charlie Barnett! Happy and eager we got out of the car, locked up, walked to the door, thick glass, painted blue with a glass tube for a handle, which we pulled open and went inside, down a short dark foyer. The hatcheck lady was in her cubicle on the left, and before we knew it, we were in. The place spread out before us.

A solid red horseshoe-shaped bar projected out from the right hand wall. Above it, same shape with red and white vertical stripes, was the bandstand. Bar and bandstand faced a tiered arrangement of chairs and tables behind low rails. Ceiling painted white, walls a dusky pink with conical-shaped lamps casting upward v-shaped rays of golden light. Gray carpeting throughout. Because food was served, the tables were set, white tablecloths, napkins, gleaming silverware, clean glasses, and in the muted light, edges and tips of silver and glass being raised or lowered, gave pleasant glints, and twinkles.

The bandstand was empty. Intermission.

We walked up five rows, where we found a table — a weeknight, not a big crowd — and sat, facing the bandstand. A waiter approached. We ordered three bottles of Falstaff, waiter disappeared, and in the thrill of it all, we looked around.

Scattered couples here and there.

But down to our left on the first tier, two tables had been pulled together. A small man with black hair graying at the temples, dark eyes, very nasty dark eyes, and under his hook nose, a hairline mustache gave accent to a sneer fighting to be a smile. In a double-breasted black and white pinstriped suit with a white carnation in his lapel, blue, monogrammed silk shirt, silver tie, gold clasp with a ruby in the center. He was smoking a cigar and it smelled good.

His left hand was around a highball, and his right arm around a young blonde, perhaps a little too pale, but for her full red lips under a cute nose and dark glasses, from top to bottom in furs and diamonds with both hands around a tall red drink with a straw, gave the joint a little class, and the bartender a headache, in his effort not to look at her, not easy, for bartenders were sly, sneaky, and enjoyed peeping. But not at her, because of the company she kept, including two other guys, big guys, in dark suits across the table, who enjoyed everything the man beside her did, and growled at everything he didn't. It seemed.

28

The waiter returned with the beers, as the band came on the stand. Charlie Barnett stood at the mike, said a few words, causing amusement, some applause, and the band began to play an upbeat arrangement based on *Gone With the Wind,* the song, not the movie.

Which we three friends enjoyed no end. Gene studied trombone since his senior year in high school, Gary had taken lessons on of all things the accordion, and I had studied trumpet, in college.

After the third round of beers, before the waiter departed, I inquired where the men's room was. The waiter pointed: Down the steps, take a left and straight ahead, which is where I went, an uneventful scene which took a most dramatic turn as I walked out, and back the way I came, with the three guys and one blonde at the table to my right, one glance at her and don't look again, an almost impossible task, for she was my age or younger, round breasted in a v-necked scarlet gown, throat snow white, magnetic, paralyzing, she didn't seem to breathe. I swung my eyes away, to my left, and up, to the bandstand—I caught my breath. Why hadn't I noticed? In large letters on the side of the bass drum, right there! My lips parted, I stared, thunderstruck, up at a smiling if not amused Jo Jones, who was looking down at me.

I stood on the gray carpeting, stopped in my tracks, listening to that great drummer, and hearing those brushes cross and recross cymbals and drums in a steady, smooth, rippling blur, like water down a mountainside.

"Hi Jo!" I grinned, waved my hand.

Jo smiled. Nodded hi. Nothing would stop those brushes. . . .

Back at the table. "That's *Jo Jones* on drums!"

"I know," Gene said, "see? On the side of the bass drum? Jo Jones?"

"Why didn't I notice?"

Gary couldn't stop laughing.

"Because you're you," Gene said.

Well, that was funny.

"But, man, he's a *great* drummer! I mean, he's groovy, he's *it!* Guys at school have his records, and he's played, *everywhere!*"

"I've got his records," Gene said.

"Do you hear that? Listen, hear those brushes?"

They listened. Gary's funnybone had been tickled by Gene's humor, and he couldn't stop laughing, and because he laughed in a hard giggle, we told him to shush, and listen, which at length he did, and we focused on the drummer, not the band, for a different kind of fun, as to do the same with the piano, or bass. Until nature called

29

Gene, and he went down the steps, and turned left as a pretty, honey-haired lady came on the stand, the band began to play, and she began to sing *I Cover the Waterfront*. Gene opened the door to the men's room. Went in. The door closed.

Gary and I sat, spellbound, listening to the singer sing, what a voice!

"It's June Christy," I whispered. "Nobody else is that good."

"It sounds like her," Gary agreed.

And Jo Jones, using his brushes across the cymbals and light stick on the snare, right there in front of us, understand, at eye level, before my return to the Army so soon, and the troopship to Germany, June Christy — she was singing to *me*! My future loomed, my eyes misted —

"Look!" Gary.

We looked. Down the stairs. The two big guys had risen from the table, and one hustled Gene to the front door, fast, while the other strode up and told us to get out.

"What do you mean!" Gary barked, like his dad.

"He means what he says," I said, and asked, "What did Gene — our friend — do?"

We rose, and in swift escort were informed that Gene had said something to the blonde.

Oh boy.

Gene, meanwhile, had been whisked outside, and as we arrived at the front door, the other guy came in from the street, without Gene.

"Come on," both guys said. "Out."

Exit Gary and one guy.

"No," I said to the other, who gazed down on me with mean, slit eyes. "Wait," I said, holding up my hand. "In two weeks I'll be on a troopship to Germany." Gathered breath, scared. "I'll leave from Hoboken, New Jersey. I won't be home for two years. Let me stay, until she finishes her song," I panted. "She's my favorite singer."

The guy paused.

"Okay."

So we stood, and listened. What a great, clear voice! How thrilled I was! *I'm watching the sea. For the one I love, to come sailing back to me* . . . but who would wait for me? Would I meet a girl who would love me, and one day await my return? but from where? Germany? No! *I* was watching the sea, to go sailing into my future, fate was calling, to tell me my fate awaited me, eyes sweeping the horizon in the beautiful voice of June Christy singing the song, in a rising wave of courage my heart beat fast: to follow my destiny into hidden places in myself, in far away lands across many rivers toward my own complete self, *she* at my side, to love me as I wanted and needed, but didn't yet know,

30

nor could understand. Tears welled in my eyes, the song was over, to scattered applause. A rough hand gripped my shoulder. Turned my body as the other hand pushed open the door, and I wiped my eyes while being shoved out onto the cold sidewalk. In a couple of blinks, however, reality returned on great big feet, as Gene and Gary, looking scared, watched me being escorted toward them, as the bodyguard (in truth), stood beside them.

Gene unlocked the door and Gary got in, reached over and opened the driver's door. Gene walked around the car, got in behind the wheel, and before I moved to get in front beside Gary, I turned to my escort.

"Thanks," I said.

The other, with icy slit eyes and a downturned mouth, made a brief nod, said,

"Beat it."

We did.

A couple of blocks away, Gene saw in the rearview mirror, the two guys, standing by the curb, watching our car as it turned onto the bridge, and headed toward St. Louis.

"What did you say to her!"

"Nothing!"

"NOTHING! *MAN! HER!*" I yelled: "HERE WE ARE! JO JONES AND JUNE CHRISTY AND CHARLIE BARNETT ARE BACK THERE, AND *WE* ARE GOING THE *OTHER* WAY!!! *WHAT DID YOU SAY?*"

Gary began to laugh.

"I know," Gene said. "I said hello, just hello. I gave a little wave —" he waved a hand over the wheel — "and said, 'Hi.' What's the matter with that?"

Gary clapped his hands over his laughing mouth. Tears ran down his cheeks, as I said,

"That was very uncool, man, dig it, that's what's the matter with that, dig you putting the cool on me not seeing Jo Jones' name on the side of his bass drum, did you see that *guy* she was with? And the two *other* guys? Didn't you know they had *guns?*"

Gene paled.

"Man! It's true!" yelled Gary. "He showed us!"

The bodyguard who had come up the steps while the other was hustling Gene outside, had said Get out, and opened the left side of his suit jacket, revealing a pistol in a holster.

That's the story.

31

In the early spring of 1956, two years later, Gene's grandma, who lived with them, died, and that summer, after a year of gradual deterioration, his father died of leukemia. In the fall, Gene himself was killed, in an air incident, while based (Navy pilot) on Bermuda. Sad, tragic story, dear friend.

His mother Mary, and brother Ed, are still alive. Mary in Dallas. Ed in a suburb somewhere in North Carolina, wife and kids. Doing well.

Gary began working as a gas station attendant outside St. Louis, and not long after married a woman of religion, no drinking, no smoking, and he has been sober ever since, a good man, and healthy, a fine father to his children and husband to his wife, although, former friends who seldom see him say he misses the old days, and yearns for someone to talk with. Too bad.

But the man who wrote this story wonders about that night, long ago, in East St. Louis. What had Jo Jones thought? of that action, taking place before his very eyes, while he kept playing, and June Christy sang?

Jo had seen Gene gesture, then speak to the beautiful little blonde, had seen the gangster's reaction, and both bodyguards rise. Exit Gene. The other came up the steps to get Gary and me, and Jo watched as we were taken to the door. Exit Gary. But I stopped, held up my hand to the bodyguard—Jo saw me!—I gestured to the singer. The bodyguard had nodded, once, and Jo had seen us stand there, side by side, until the end of her song, so beautiful it was, and profound, but not complete until the writing of this, to see from Jo's point of view while he was playing his drums. So, with that as the reason, let this story be in his memory. The smile he gave me was genuine, above his brushes, crossing and recrossing as she sang, the drummer in action like the wind, water down a mountainside, the blue in the sky.

The Fourth Surprise

ON THE FLOOR of a canyon with glass and steel walls, a man struggled through a blizzard. His coat collar was up, watch cap rolled down over his ears, shoulders hunched against the white blast. His gloved hands were in fists. He was not altogether sober, and as he crossed the avenue watching his step, a gust of wind whipped him clean of snow and almost knocked him down: eyes stinging in the steady, horizontal fury. In part blinded, and staggering, he crossed the avenue — auto traffic minimal and at a crawl — and stepping up onto the sidewalk, discerned in the darkness, for it was night, the shadowed figure of a snow-covered bum, eating frozen garbage out of a corner trash container. Crossing to the figure, he saw the bum was young, and that he had no gloves, hands trembling from the cold as he had wiped snow from and finished what appeared to be the last of a crust of pizza.

*   *   *

In retrospect, the man decided he would have done what he had no matter his condition, in the spirit of Christmas, and Christmas three days away, men, he reasoned, do deeds out of the ordinary, and to give the bum his gloves, which were new, had been bought on credit, was an act of charity in the mood of the season, although, in the face of a different and unanticipated storm ahead, the one awaiting him at home, on top of it all, the bum hadn't wanted them.

He had taken off his gloves, handed them to the bum, who was wiping his lips with the raggedy cuff of his army coat.

"No," the bum said. "You keep 'em."

"But your hands are freezing!"

Shrug.

"Here."

"Well," the bum said, "why not?" Grinned. "Thanks." Put the gloves on, looked down at them, and shuffled off into the storm.

The first surprise was the bum was young, and the second, too late, gift received with an existential "Why not?" baffled the giver, who made his way home dark in mind, yet in spirit trying to be pleased he had done a good deed. He was therefore divided, and when he walked into his kitchen, saw her reading the paper at the table, and she glanced at his hands and asked where his gloves were, and he told her, he received his third surprise, a sobering one, to match the weather.

But the fourth surprise awaited them both.

Meanwhile, tempest.

If, she said, being part Irish, with indigenous temper, the bum didn't want them why did you give them to him and why tell me he didn't want them, you *know* what I'd think, why tell the truth? why not say you gave your gloves to a bum in the spirit of Christmas? and NOT tell me he didn't *want* them! Brand new on your charge card. We decided, remember, not to have a tree this year because we're broke, and you give away a pair of new gloves to a bum who didn't want them, twelve dollars plus tax and interest down the pipe and we have no tree. Great. Why didn't you say he was glad? and grateful?

Truth, she had often said, like San Francisco, was overrated, and as her eyes got hard, and her lips thin, prosecution was winning the case, and defense was defensive. So, blockhead that he was, thinking to play it as she admitted she did — no defense like a good offense — he said that as a matter of fact he didn't like the gloves, and it didn't matter.

"If it didn't matter," she said, face pale, "why did you buy them?"

"I'll get another pair."

"When?"

"Tomorrow."

"On your charge card?"

"Sure," and he did two things that surprised him: he shrugged, and then said, "Why not?"

"I'll tell you why not," she said.

Oh, ho ho ho, ha ha ha, and after she finished, he explained, trying to be reasonable, which didn't work — she had been with him during the purchase — yet he was a fiend for details, and the gloves had a spring clip attached to each cuff so when not being worn could be clipped together in a manufacturing designer's gimmick, in case of loss, had he thought and he should have, he knew the retail — and wholesale — business, lest the purchaser lose one glove, attach them together, just in case — and maybe lose both. Anyway the gloves were stiff, it had been a bother with metal clips hanging out in the cold, to sting his wrists, creating an impulse to pull shirt cuffs down as liners.

"Unh huh," she said. "Some Christian you are. Give away a pair of gloves you didn't want, to a bum, the poor guy. Why didn't you give them to me?" Pause. "Or to the thrift shop?"

34

His one way out was to look inward and realize another unconscious act, and, as she said, he'd used the bum to unload unwanted
gloves, as people did with slaves, to lessen the fact of slavery, so, to
match this sad fact, he had but his resolve to not do it again, not an
easy task, because it was built into the culture, and to not be unconscious was to attempt to change what was given at birth: an elitist
racism, and to realize, he realized, that he, of all people, had found
his victim, and the one way to freedom for both was first, that he
henceforth identify the other person as another person, and second,
consider his motive, and third, form a clear-headed decision on which
to act, as the foundation of his resolve, and bring a ray of light to
a dark and needy world.

In this way he learned. One never stopped learning. And yet,
from another, more forgiving point of view, there was a poor young
man wearing a pair of good gloves, walking the freezing streets of
a huge, and often uncaring city, and his hands were warm.

*   *   *

The next day, true to his word, the man returned to the store,
charge card in wallet, and wallet in pocket, ready for retail action.

The main floor was busy, atmosphere and bustle festive in colorful decorations to match the season, yet in its contained landmark
character — a large building in the fashionable center of town, on one
of the great, and elegant avenues of the world — its mood was low key,
and the loud, the rude, and the flashy had the city before them to
shop in, as they preened, and displayed themselves, and didn't bother
to shop here.

He rather meandered toward the glove counter, enjoying the sight
of clothes in another part, the men's section, and dreaming of money
as his gaze fell to rest on expensive imported topcoats, jackets, shoes,
and suits of great variety, in the muted atmosphere, for the floor was
carpeted, and the salesmen professionals, elegant themselves, with
sharp, cool eyes, waiting for bait with thin lips, although later, at the
bar after work, they were raucous, and vulgar, like strange children.

He bought a new pair of gloves which he liked, for around the
same price, from a poised and courteous salesman.

"Will this be cash, sir, or charge?"

"Charge."

Out came the card, bam! signed his name, received card and
carbon copy of the receipt, and left the store wearing his purchase.

Walked downtown, noticing the sun was lower in the sky than he thought, so he quickened his pace, because he had a plan, and because the blizzard had lost its punch during the night, and the sun had come out, weather warmed, snow turned cold slush, and in his boots he didn't have to watch his step, so he got where he wanted to go pretty fast, and on arrival, standing right there, fifty feet away, in front of him, was the fourth surprise, and he stopped, thunderstruck.

As in other parts of the country, on certain days farmers drove their trucks into cities and set up tables in neighborhood locations, differing according to the day. Today was Saturday, and hoping not to be late for the apple people, who left early, he saw, in the center of the midway, on the edge of a large city park, as a vision—being something of an artist he knew a vision when he saw one—fifty feet away, between the long line of vendors on the left, and on the right, beyond which the empty spot of Mister Caradonna and His Apple Family meaning they had left. No apples today! He saw the young woman who drove the produce truck with her brothers and father. She was rosy-cheeked, very pretty, in boots and jeans, a bright red, lined jacket, hood flung back, and her dark hair free. She stood facing the man with his new gloves, her legs and feet braced, her right, gloved hand outstretched, just as her left, each holding a seven foot Christmas tree. Her dark eyes gleamed as she grinned, as she recognized the man as a customer, and cried out—

"TAKE WHICHEVER ONE YOU WANT! THEY'RE FREE! MERRY CHRISTMAS! COME ON!"

In sustained, if not disciplined, disbelief, he drew closer, and asked—

"Is it true?" with a smile.

"Sure! Which one do you want?"

Each year these people brought tall pines from the country, with a starting price of twenty dollars, so, heart in mouth, he made his choice, meeting her sparkling eyes, his tree in hand, he made a low laugh in his throat, and with a grin—

"You don't know what this means." Pause. "Thanks, a lot. Merry Christmas."

She nodded, and as he turned away, to go home, on that Saturday, of that year, two days before Christmas, with a tree, he heard her outcries for the last one, COME ON! IT'S FREE! and he couldn't wait to go up the stairs, open the door, and go in, tree in hand—gloved hand, and say Okay, look at this! and relate, to his no doubt amazed and happy loved-one, his story of celestial reimbursement, to which she would say Oh you, and that's what he did, you betcha, and that's what she said, with a bit more, before they fell silent, placed

36

the tree in the metal tripod by the rear window, and began to string the lights. Then hang the bright, and haunting blue, green, gold and silver planets, and arrange the spire on top, then angels, funny toys from yesteryear, little animals, nestling among branches, and tinsel last of all. The lights winked on. They stood away, hand in hand, looking at it, shining and twinkling before them, reflected in the darkening window: a magic sight to see.

End of a Dream

IN A FREIGHT CAR of a moving train, he saw a steamship trunk at the far end, lid thrown open, I saw a black man's head rise in terror, and stare at me, as I approached him. I too was black. I lunged, caught his head in my hands, my head in my hands in a motion as I bent over staring up at me. I slapped a lethal bottlecap on the back of my head, struggling to be free. Trapped in the trunk. Helpless. An electric jolt blasted my brain — I sprang back, and turned.

A dark figure spread-eagled in the open door of the freight car said I would never get off alive.

The landscape raced by.

I smelled fresh air, hay, clover, the sky was blue above green fields, but I couldn't jump. He was there, and the train was going fast as the dark figure advanced toward me — it wasn't me. But I was in his power, and woke in his embrace.

Over There

THE GRAY LINE of refugees trickled toward the horizon, illusionary in dawn's mist. White smoke crept over black craters between shattered silver stumps of trees, and silent, cool brown mud.

Overhead, in the blue sky, a biplane appeared, and keeping its altitude, circled the marchers, perhaps making up its mind whether or not to descend, and machinegun them, but in a happier move, the plane straightened, found a new course, and flew out of view.

The naked man stood before the other man who held the pistol. It was not known if he too was naked, although it seemed so.

The naked man smiled, as if he knew what was coming, as he would welcome it, and appeared amused as the other pulled the trigger, shot him through the heart, paused, and fired again.

Following another pause, he fired twice more. Two shots, same place, because he had appeared living again, and he thought he had killed him.

Double Vision — *The Rewrite*

A FAT MAN in a plaid suit walked west on 23rd Street, passing the quiet bar where Ritter sat, drink in hand.

"I saw him on the bus to work. This morning," the bartender said, her eyes intent. "72nd Street, Central Park West."

Ritter turned, looked out the window. The fat man wasn't there.

"This morning," Ritter said, "a guy in a gray suit and vest passed my building."

"This afternoon," he continued, in restaurant scent of garlic, ketchup, french fries and sizzling chops, "I saw him again, walking west, on 20th Street."

Blue skies.

Fingertips on glass.

In muted outside auto traffic, icy vodka.

Daffodil yellow.

Fan Letter

Green Turtle Cay
Bahamas   12/8/85

Fielding,

[Musial,] I find in brackets, in the book where the author describing a childhood baseball game, he grew up in Missouri, mentioned the then star, and so she marks this in ink — she knows about books — and then later still I notice on the bookmark that came in the book she lent me, she'd been using a grocery receipt for $15.23, paid for with a twenty, $4.77 change, has written on the back, in ink, "Musial."

September in the Rain

HE KNELT in the rain. At the foot of the statue of Lincoln, in Union Square: Saturday, September 22, 1979.

His Uncle Essex had died three days before. Old, very ill, and it was, as all agreed, a blessing. But the real cause?

This is the real cause.

The rain drove down, and drenched him, as he prayed.

Asking for an image.

He snapped his fingers: *give me. Give me.*

Raised his head: in the distance, and behind Lincoln, superimposed over Broadway — looking uptown — a triangle of green and gold dotted lines hung in the rain: from the corner of Uncle Essex's desk up to the model airplane hung on a thread from the ceiling, to himself as a boy, gazing upward, at the plane, that he had built with his father, two years before his father had died, in April, 1942. And Uncle Essex kept the boy alive in a creative faith that would be Essex's undoing.

He and Frances had worked for almost twenty years, before they were married, having saved their money, for their dream: way west of St. Louis, a house in the middle of a field with trees, on top of a hill, surrounded by farm country. There was a grape arbor, a garden with tomatoes as big as softballs. A pond with frogs and lily pads, willow trees at one end. Rose bushes, flower gardens with neat green grass that the young poet cut, each Saturday, peanut butter with lettuce and tomato sandwiches, cool milk, the best he ever had, before, or since, as his aunt Frances smiled, in their kitchen. A bird feeder outside the large, front picture window facing east, where a hundred kind of birds, including chickadees, flew and fluttered in, so too the bully bluejays, like fate, cardinals everywhere, it seemed, the whole team, and ever mindful of the needs of others, in less than the span whereby a seed becomes a sapling, Aunt Frances's sister fell ill, then very ill, and begged her to return, to care for her, which, it is a horror to report, they did. They sold their dream house, on top of the hill. Pond, trees, flowers, garden, home, all. They had called it Essex Field.

And in less than the span it takes a sapling to become a tree, her sister died, and her other sister fell ill. Then very ill, and vicious, a whimpering, self-pitying dictator, she took too long to die, she hardened, and at last went cold. But too late for Essex! First his body rebelled, in illnesses meaning surgery. Next his mind, and a new word came in beginning with s, for a poor rhyme with finality.

Two days after he died, the two lovers walked across the city to the Vanguard, to hear Red Garland, and as Red played piano and they listened, the adult poet realized many things had changed, and many more were on the way, but on *They Didn't Believe Me,* his blood changed because his heart was melting. Tears stung his eyes.

Later, in a nearby bar something was wrong. She knew he was sad, he didn't say anything, and he talked about that song, and she knew nobody believed how he felt, not because they wouldn't, but because there wasn't anybody in New York who could, who, for that matter, anywhere, anywhere in the world could know? to be able to believe him, even in 1938.

It had begun to rain. Hard. They said so long to the bartender, and left. Heads down, collars up, walking north, uptown. Crossed 14th Street, and as they were going parallel with Union Square, he wanted an image, and said so. She said okay.

They walked into the Square. She sat on a bench. Watched him cross to the statue of Lincoln, and kneel down. Saw him snap his fingers. Look up, as if seeing something. She rose, walked over, stood behind him, followed his gaze up Broadway. Nothing. She stepped aside, glanced down. His faced was raised, lips parted, eyes focused, expression radiant.

On the way home he told her, about the green and gold triangle in the air. Uncle Essex's desk, the plane, Essex's stamp collection, homemade camera, the death of his father, and of Essex himself, and Frances, and Essex Field, and the sad, sad story, but as he talked about the radio, *I Love a Mystery,* Edward R. Murrow and England at war, she saw he was at war, like the plane: suspended in a dive — she saw the boy on the floor at his uncle's feet, just as she had seen the man kneel at the foot of the statue of Lincoln, seeing it as if it was being unveiled before her, the radio was on the windowsill above the tool chest, the dial was lighted, the boy sat cross-legged as his uncle smoked Wings cigarettes and slid stamps into celluloid folders, there was music, a dramatic narrative voice, and action superimposed over the vista of Essex Field, tears welled in her eyes, she gripped his arm, moving close to him as she wept, in the complete, full force of life, soaked to the skin, together, walking home in the rain.

The Planets

IN THE SPRING of 1953, three young men, good friends, walked from East 10th Street to West 52nd Street, to hear some music at a nightclub called Le Downbeat.

As they went in the front door they saw Stan Getz and Bobby Brookmeyer playing to an empty house, but they played like the joint was jammed, with such conviction if one closed one's eyes, the place *was* jammed. But both eyes open there was nobody there save the bartender who served the young men beer. Having paid, they sipped, tapped their feet to the swift, neat melodic interplay of tenor saxophone and trombone, maybe a little too sweet, but a trademark anyway, to the three young men, unthinkable, these days, that no one else was there.

One of the young men said,

"That's Tommy Potter on bass, Roy Haynes on drums and Al Haig on piano."

Oh *man! Wow! Dig* it!

The bar was about twenty feet long, to the left of the front door. At the far end, up some five steps, a small bandstand.

The place itself was like a long, rather wide, hallway, the restaurant section at the far end, rear wall, under a high ceiling. Tables in rows. Neat white tablecloths, napkins, glasses and silverware sparkled. Chairs snug, looked upholstered. It had a silver-draped, polished-mirror, upholstered-blue luxury liner effect, heightened in the far left corner, way in the back, where a flight of carpeted steps led up to a shadowed balcony with a white railing, beyond which, against its rear wall, a long white sofa was flanked by upholstered chairs and chrome cigarette stands.

People came in, had a drink, listened a while, and left.

Al Haig's head was down, face averted, right ear almost on the keyboard. His hands moved left and right, fingers dancing on the keys: seized a rung of music, climbed up and down a ladder of sound.

The young men were impressed, sipped beer, snapped their fingers, tapped their feet, nodding their heads to the beat, fixing on Al Haig, and his hard, fast bop piano on the very edge of percussion.

The front door opened. A couple of guys came in.

The three young men turned. Not prepared for what they saw

or, for that matter, what would follow, in Le Downbeat.

A very large, plump white man in a worn gray suit over a clean white t-shirt, leather shoes, who looked like an M.D. hasbeen, speaking in soft, pleading tones to the small, slender, young black man at his side, dressed in a threadbare dark suit, frayed white shirt open at the collar, scuffed leather shoes. He seemed not to have slept in a week, and each day was a trial. His head was up, as on a shelf, eyes wide, lips parted in a way like a puzzled infant, not quite seeing the world, but as a man, young as he was, he'd seen too much, was a down and out wreck, a little stooped, and bitter, sad, angry, disgusted, bugged, and very very stoned.

"Miles," the white guy said, frowning, "will you take care of yourself? Please?"

Miles growled, "Yeah."

"I mean it. Will you be okay?"

Harsh whisper. "Yeah."

"Promise?"

"Unh huh." Laryngitis. "I promise. You can go."

So the big guy, with a worried look, watched Miles walk to the bar, and sit on a barstool next to the third young man, at whom the big guy looked, in an expectant way, and the young man, baffled, didn't know what to do, think of it — he knew who Miles was, he had the records — and there Miles was, sitting beside him, and he missed the message the big guy was giving him: would *he* take care of Miles?

Complete confusion.

The big guy left.

The young guys looked at each other, in particular at the third young man who was gazing down at Miles, seated — slumped, on the barstool beside him. Stan Getz, Bobby Brookmeyer, Roy Haynes, Tommy Potter and Al Haig slamming away, Miles raised his head, and as he looked up at the young man, gestured with his right thumb at the bandstand, to keep the young man laughing for the rest of his life, in that grating, gruff whisper, Miles asked:

"Who's that?"

The three young men, about to laugh, checked it, not altogether sure if they should, for the glance from Miles held such deep wickedness it was difficult to interpret, it had come in a flicker and gone in a wink: he had seen them about to laugh, and stop, so he turned away and looked across, up at the roaring bandstand, then down at the bar. Cool, bop humor.

The set came to an end.

It was not known how Miles made it up and onto the bandstand, but there he was, and things got going, except he couldn't find the mouthpiece. It was on the trumpet, right where it should be, but his lips couldn't find it, everybody behind him blasting away, yet how strange! Tommy Potter, Roy Haynes and Al Haig had stayed on the stand, to back up Miles or so it appeared — there they were! As Miles found it, breathing light and easy, his fantastic lyric character, uneven, a little lost, that night, but tart, and pure: *The Way You Look Tonight*.

It couldn't last.

But for a while.

Next thing they knew, he was walking down the steps, off the stand, and listen to this. He turned left, walked the length of the whole joint, the place deserted, clear back, up the steps onto the rear balcony, and sat on the long white sofa, slumped to his left, his head landing bam in the lap of a seated, beautiful, she was incredible, Swedish blonde with pageboy bangs, in a long white gown. She put her hand on the back of his head. Getz, Brookmeyer, Tommy Potter, Roy Haynes and Al Haig were blasting away. The blonde stared down the length of the place, over the heads of the young men at the bar and out the front door above 52nd Street, above New York City, beyond the North American Continent and off the edge of the world into endless, galactic space, where planets whirled, and suns burned, yet also seemed to twinkle, to living music, played live, to be heard forever. And ever.

Al Haig died of a heart attack on November 16, 1982. He was 58. He had played everywhere, with everybody. Was influenced by Teddy Wilson, Nat Cole and Bud Powell.

Full Circle

THE SAME NIGHT after Miles had spoken with the odd young man in the powdered wig, at the bar in the Cafe Bohemia, the young poet came in around midnight, and had a bottle of beer, at the bar. Remained standing, listening to Miles, Coltrane, Red Garland, Paul Chambers, and Philly Joe make music he had not just never heard before, but couldn't believe he was hearing. They were getting better and better and better.

He was very poor in those days, often going for two and three days without food. He rolled his own cigarettes and could live for a week on a dollar, as A&P eggs were 49¢ a dozen, margarine 10¢ a stick, a loaf of bread 29¢ and a dime for a sack of Bull Durham tobacco which came with two packets of cigarette papers free. But to hear Miles, he bummed and begged — and worked — for a couple of dollars: there wasn't a cover or minimum at the Bohemia, and a bottle of beer, which cost a dollar, in sips, lasted at least two sets.

Imagine being a poet, sipping from a bottle of beer, while listening to those guys take their solos and come in strong together at the end. To open, Miles began, John next, then Red, Paul and Philly Joe, imagine it, alive, *live music,* the place not crowded on weeknights, music! giving life to love, and liberty to rhythm tapping his feet he closed his eyes, hearing Miles and Coltrane tear the front door off, on Miles' farewell to Charlie Parker: *Bye Bye Blackbird,* with those three great aces backing them up.

He stood about a third of the way down the bar. Didn't sit. He knew how to listen to music, and he was listening to this music in that way of hearing new work that the opening outward of the inner ear does something to balance. In suspense hearing nothing but music, there was nothing but music, anywhere, he was up in a world and the world was music.

The beginning of this tune went by so fast he didn't recognize it, not that they played it so fast, no, it was so familiar he missed what it was, and being smart enough not to listen back to get it, and miss what was going on, he followed, and that's why what happened had such an impact, because he was altogether inside the music — to anticipate Miles was impossible and he had tried — while smoking dope and listening to records with his pal John Chamberlain — so, on this song, once again the elusive Miles Davis got away by keeping in front, and as everybody knew, as everyone knows, hearing it live and on record — well. That night this song went on forever, on and on, the tables, glassware, chairs, barstools seemed to dance, leaving the crowd stunned, and before the young man knew it, Miles was doing what he always did: walked over to stand beside each of the other four as each took their solo, so in a wink, Miles was standing, facing Philly Joe Jones, Miles snapping his fingers, holding his trumpet at his side, would the ceiling collapse? Philly Joe! Before his eyes, perhaps the poet had had a lapse, Miles was center stage between the overhead red spotlights, beside Coltrane, raised his trumpet to his lips, Coltrane's tenor raised — they all five hit together, in 16ths, for about ten seconds, in the perfect, very funny, even zany, melody, of *Billy Boy,* and Aunty Mary laughed.

Miles

THE WAY it had all begun was he heard that Miles Davis had a quintet that was playing in the Village, at the Cafe Bohemia.

So one evening he went over, heard two sets and came out ears ringing, starry-eyed and weak in the knees.

He had never, but never, heard anything like that, ever, *any*where, and it didn't take him a few days to recover, no, because he never did recover, for there was no recovery, this was permanent.

A college pal had gone into publishing pamphlets, very esoteric stuff, classy formats, limited editions in a series, one of which, in the fall of 1955, had been a booklet of eight of his poems. An edition of 150 copies from which he received 25 copies as payment, and after the four seasons had passed by twice, he had only two copies left. There were no more. That, was that.

In the area below 14th Street where he lived, in those days, he often encountered older artists who lived in the neighborhood. They would stop and talk, or go into The Colony, have coffee or beer, and talk or, more like it, he would listen, to them. He wanted to see, and be seen looking. The painter he most wanted to see him was Philip Guston, who was himself difficult to see, so often distracted or depressed the young man knew not what to say. Against his youthful, and demanding will, seeing Philip Guston on the street, Philip passed him by, not seeing him, which disappointed, depressed, hurt and pissed the young poet off. Although he knew that Philip, having painted all day, took afternoon breaks. Went to the movies. What he saw while watching the screen is not known, but images appeared in his later work that suggest possibilities. He emerged from the movie house so distracted and dazed anybody who knew him knew enough to avoid him: he had a house of cards inside a circle of dominoes in his head, to at last clear up the meaning of the initials PG on movie ads and billboards: *You will see strange figures and objects involving indiscretion and an odd violence.*

One morning, around noon, the young poet awoke and realized the person who would see him and most understand his poetry *was* Philip Guston, and after breakfast, in a kind of fervor, he dressed, took in hand the next to last copy of his booklet, left his building and

55

walked down to 10th Street. Found the address. Walked up the steps, you could do that then, didn't have to phone first. Knocked on the studio door. No answer. Guston wasn't there. Maybe he's at a movie. Poet disappointed.

Sat on the stairs and thought, and having a pencil with him, wrote a brief note on the flyleaf and signed his name, nickname, rather — Philip knew him. He put the booklet on the floor, and leaned it against the bottom of the studio door.

Walking home it was okay and good, but it wasn't complete. He wanted to give it to Philip.

"Here. This is for you. I hope you like it."

The next to last copy!

Panic!

No!

An about face, ran back praying Philip was still at the movie. Ran up the stoop, in the door, up the steps and there it was where he'd left it. Picked it up, went down the stairs, out the door, down the stoop to the sidewalk bang met a pal. They went to The Colony, had a few beers.

That evening, in another bar, still with his next to last copy, while talking with friends he fell into reverie, realizing the Miles Davis Quintet was right across town, and in a little while, why not go over, hear some music, and give Miles the booklet? The pencil in his pocket had an eraser, so erase the note to Philip (he'll be sorry) and write in a new note to Miles? Swell! Erase the nickname, sign his proper name! No sooner thought than done.

Standing at the bar in the Bohemia, having erased as best he could, he wrote a note to Miles Davis and signed his name. But he was nervous and self-conscious. Scared. Things were tough enough on Miles, the place was so racist. The Italian gangsters talked — if they talked — with their tongues glued behind their teeth. Skin drained gray, eyes dead: they saw you, they saw you dead. Their bodies were full, and lumpy, stuffed with meat, bread and blood and a twisting sense of humor. One stood near the men's room, a living humanoid of mutilation with heavy-lidded rattlesnake eyes, thick, gray slabs of cheeks, gray suit, green shirt, brown tie, so that as the set ended, the five black musicians had to pass him, to go outside for a smoke.

The way that guy looked at them almost made the young man ill, yet his anger at the injustice — the rape of their creative intelligence in a racist killer's sneer — kept him alert. Plus, in the poet's hunger for life, he knew the musicians knew why that gangster was, oh yes, that was part of the music! Who else ran the clubs?

Sure enough, the set was over. The five men came down off the

56

stage to applause, and made their way to the front door.

The area along the bar was wide enough—beyond the barstools—to walk in twos, passing both restrooms, heading toward the hat/coat checkroom by the front door. In the space between, the thug leaned against the wall, on an angle away from the young poet, standing at the bar nervous as he was, without that goon being there, and as the musicians approached, the gangster regarded them with the contempt he held for obvious victims. Each of the five men set his face in mask: one peek behind, into the volcano.

"Excuse—excuse me, Miles?" the young poet stammered, as the mobster drifted away, back toward the service end of the bar. The poet held out the booklet. "I'd like—I'd like to give this to you."

The five men stopped.

"What is it?" Miles asked. His great voice.

"A book, a booklet, of poems, a-a-eight poems I wrote."

"Are you a writer?"

Pause. "A poet."

Miles said to the others, they could go outside, he'd be out in a minute.

As they went, Miles accepted the gift, thanking the young man, not much younger than himself, and opening the cover to the flyleaf, read the inscription.

"Thank you," Miles said again, holding up a hand. "I'll give it to the bartender, to keep for me." His expression was complex because he was accepting something while on his way outside, where they waited, and he would have to go back before he could go out, which the poet understood, and watched, as Miles went back down the bar and gave it to the bartender, speaking in a low voice, the bartender nodded. Miles returned, seeing the other eager to say something more. Eager, and agitated.

"May I—Miles! May I say one more thing? I know you're on break, and—"

"Sure," Miles said. "It's okay."

"Oh—oh, *man,* I studied trumpet in college, I didn't get very far, I was drafted, but I I mean I listened to your records and, I mean, I hear what you're doing, and you're great, Miles, you're *great!*"

Miles looked at him.

"And I know this is crazy, my asking you this, but the poet Robert Creeley, in his new book, in the introduction, he says his poetic line follows your melodic line, on *But Not for Me.* His line—his poetic line—"

Gruff. Yeah! "I get it. Sounds good!"

"Could I ask you, to, and of course this is im-impossible but, is there a chance, wu-would you, play it for me?"

Miles smiled, but shook his head.

"The numbers are decided beforehand." Seeing deep embarrassment added, "I'm sorry." And walked outside.

Well, the poet sighed, embarrassed, self-conscious, dismayed, and angry at himself, yet understanding the professional situation, arrived at peace of mind in the happy thought that he had given Miles the booklet, and! in a pre-Egyptian, sculpted burnished blackened bronze, how handsome Miles was, to deepen the image, and add to the already profound.

Sipping beer he realized he was far ahead of himself without knowing it, because those five guys had walked by him going out, and they would walk by again coming in, and in the way of his awareness of FIVE *GREAT* MUSICIANS, his spirit took off, sure enough, there they were, walking right by him on the way to the stage, next they were on the stage, next with instruments in hand: Miles's trumpet. Coltrane's tenor. Philly Joe's sticks. Red's hands above the keys and Paul poised above catgut, but not yet, no, because Miles said something to John, crossed stage to Paul, spoke with him. Next with Philly Joe, back to Red, a murmured message. Miles, standing between the two red cones of light, having put his dark glasses on, he raised his muted trumpet, as Red with both hands, Paul cool on bass and Philly Joe set the beat, they came in together with Miles, as never before, and never again, played the soft, poetic, no vibrato, ever dancing melody on a muted horn: *But Not for Me.*

Followed by Coltrane.

Wow.

Not an easy tale to tell at a party or a bar. In fact forbidden, except to the most perceptive friends, in no less than the perfect setting, as he discovered the hard way. Ever mistaken for a story about Miles Davis being a nice guy after those other stories, or, for one of a young poet who gave a great trumpet player a booklet, and the musician played the song requested.

Somewhere along the line, no doubt early on, Miles had his variation of Aunty Mary. So, beyond his knowledge, through her (or him — an uncle!), he shared a kinship with the poet.

His lyric went around his rage and gave him a foundation for expression — beauty, wit, tenderness, and fear, and helplessness — which included the Aunty Mary figure by paying homage to her, while feeling the exact opposite.

His gift, that of the classic lyric, no matter how he felt, *for any reason,* was thus a curse, and the reason why, in the doll jokes of the day, he was described as the Miles Doll. Wind him up and he turns his back on you, before a full house in London. Yes! Turned his back on the audience, began to play, and continued to play, and the English were oh well very very. This was on his European tours late that fall, and the following spring. His star was becoming a comet.

Late that next spring, almost summer, the Quintet returned, and opened up at the Bohemia. The happy evenings of just a few people at the bar, and scattered couples at tables, where you heard every note, were gone. The house wasn't packed, but it was full, and the ugly days of down and out Miles, were also gone. He looked great. Stovepipe pants and raglan sleeves. The group was red hot, they played patterns of music as complex as Schoenberg. Coltrane followed Miles in grand, rising howls and outcries peaked with a scream, dropped three octaves to the melody, Red, Paul and Philly Joe spread out a background galaxy, Coltrane had all the space he wanted, and Miles stood beside him, trumpet in left hand, snapping the fingers on his right, head a little down, as he listened.

It kept going, and going, and going. Better and better. Polished to an enamel surface against blue electricity, which Miles kept rough on the edges: never before, music like that. Never again. The night they played *Billy Boy,* and Aunty Mary had laughed, the audience applauded. The young poet was speechless, his whole body tingling, felt himself begin to crumble, and the set was over. The five masters came off the stage, and in a bit of a crush accepted compliments from fans, and made their way outside.

"Miles, *Miles!*" cried the poet. "BILLY BOY! *The best yet!* Man, I have *never,* EVER HEARD *ANYTHING*—LIKE IT!"

Clapped his hand over his mouth, and turned away. Good God— in this crowd Miles had his hands full, *leave him alone!* Yet Miles had seen him, and in fact was pleased, but the poet, filled with self-loathing, would he *never* learn to shut up? Couldn't he have said, Excuse me, before he spoke, or just said, Great, Miles. Great. Why all the blah blah BLAH *BLAH BLAH BLAH*! but felt someone touch him, he turned, and there was Miles, smiling, his hand on the poet's shoulder, Miles' eyes direct, understanding, and warm, as he said, It's okay,

"I've still got the book."

Kid Stuff
A Novel, in Outline with Notes

for Pat

"Try as I like to find the way,
I never can get back by day,
Nor can remember plain and clear
The curious music that I hear."

—Robert Louis Stevenson
The Land of Nod

Chapter One: *The Deep Sleep*

MAY.
The second Thursday.
The window was open.
A moon.
He kissed him.
In shadows.
In bed.
A little kiss. A test kiss.
Voices. Excited whispers.
"Do you like it?"
"I don't know." Pause. "Do you?"
"I think so. Let's try again!"
"No!"
"Why?"
"It's crazy! *Kissing*! Guys don't kiss!"
"I know. But we've done everything else." Pause. "Almost."
"This is crazy."
"Don't you like it?"

"Yes, but don't *talk* about it!"

"Okay."

"I'm scared."

"Me too. But—"

"No kissing."

"Okay. You feel good. Do you want to?"

"—Yes!"

They did.

And afterwards he got out of bed, put on his underpants, jeans, t-shirt, and sneakers. Crossed the room, climbed out the window, dropped to the lawn below.

Keeping in shadows made his way to the house next door: climbed up the trellis and entered a second-storey window. Turned, looked back at the house, where the other was. They waved. Went to bed. Slept the deep sleep of secret lovers in the river of yesterday, sweeping today into the ocean of tomorrow, at seventeen.

Chapter Two: *What Brenda Saw*

IN THE HOUSE across the street, Brenda Baxter, kneeling on the rug at her (second-storey) window (open), lowered her infra-red binoculars, clenched her fists, and groaned. Helpless. There: across the street from whom she termed "her" shortstop, who lived next door to "her" second baseman, both of whom she had seen that day, in school, emerge from the boys' lavatory into the deserted corridor, touching each other in a way she couldn't believe. His voice low—

"My room. Tonight."

Didn't see her come around the corner. Saw her!

"Bren!"

"Hi."

All three blushed crimson, and after hasty lies, in silence went their ways. Three young people, late for class.

She wanted to be in that room with them, and she wanted to scream and laugh and go berserk. Flung herself onto her bed, buried her face in a pillow and wept laughter, as the novelist leaned back from his typewriter and looked at what he had written. He sighed, and picked up his notes. Routine novelistic formula. He had a chapter with a scene he couldn't wait to write. Brenda, with her best friend, Virgil Eager, buying the binoculars, she not telling him why—

"It's a surprise."

A surprise! The roots of her hair tingled and her body got hot, seeing again in her mind *by pure chance* she'd looked out her window, and saw the light in his room go on, then off, but in that flash, what she had seen! Oh God! The best double play combination in all-county high school baseball, *naked*! In an embrace!

Her hands trembled.

Virgil was baffled.

What she had seen and wanted to see more of, must remain a secret. School was almost over, everybody would graduate, and after long summer vacations in the country or by the sea, in the fall, off to colleges and universities. If word got out, meanwhile, she vowed it wouldn't be through her. Wasn't easy, keeping such a hot secret secret. Habit-formed to tell Virgil everything, he had always been cool. Wasn't the talking type anyway, rather a quiet person with a daffy personality.

Having noticed her distraction, that day, after school he breezed by her locker, where she stood, thinking what books to take home.

"Hi baby," he said. Leaned close, tilting his snap-brim hat, so no one could see, as other kids watched, he murmured, "May I take you to a dirty movie?"

"Virgil," she whispered, smiling. Looked up at him, "No! Come downtown with me. I have to buy something."

"What?"

"You'll see."

"I see you standing before me."

"As I see you, yet you still shall see."

Patterns of dialogue.

"Okay." Began to dance.

A tall skinny boy, shoulders broad and waist narrow, milky skin, wispy black hair, ascetic features: droopy, dark brown eyes, an arched nose above red, rosebud lips.

Day after day. Black and white double-breasted pinstripe suit. White shirt, unironed, open at the collar, and often casting his face in shadow: a dark gray, snap-brim hat, with a narrow, pale yellow band, and a small red feather, set on an angle. He had big feet. Black leather wingtip shoes. White silk socks, with a vertical row of tiny black diamonds up the ankles. Couple dozen pair.

He danced down the corridor, students stood aside, amused, for they knew him. Fred Astaire bowed out the side door of the building. Brenda selected books, put them in her book bag, closed the locker door, slipped the lock in, clicked it shut and spun the dial.

Walked toward the same door Virgil had used, opened it and stepped outside, and as it closed behind her, she walked down the driveway toward the far field, seeing him there: seated on the low worn, wooden bench, like a long, lanky, moody bird, not far from third base. The hardball diamond: the team had begun to practice.

In view of the action to follow, the novelist blocked out in mental and written notes, some background.

Virgil had been in part raised an orphan, after his father left home. Mother very ill. He and his little brother were sent to a home for boys until mom got better. She did. And back home with her, Virgil entered seventh grade, his brother, what happened to his brother? Who knows? The novelist frowned, and considered the brother's reason for existing in fiction. Get the father away so Virgil is dependent on his mother (thus his near-desperate need for Brenda). Yet although she—his mom—is home, is better, yet still ill. Virgil has to in part take care of her, and work at jobs in the evenings for the obvious novelistic reasons, and his little brother, this Dickens nonsense, dies. How? Later. This is the *plot*! Forcing Virgil even closer to his mother (and Brenda), so as she, Brenda, leaves the ball diamond after that (upcoming) game with the two infielders she's been spying on, Virgil is devastated. Brenda doesn't realize the impact until too late.

Psychology easy. Bren's an only child. Not spoiled in a bad way, but she's used to getting what she wants. Her last name, Baxter, tells the rest. Mom's a housewife and dad's an executive (be fun to make him a successful copywriter, but that's too close to the typewriter, and me, he thought, behind it). An exec for a firm in the retail biz. Baxter.

To get to the bridge, or central transition of the novel, involves five points of concern:

1: Description of Brenda.

2: The game where something funny happens at second base (figure that out), before Brenda walks off the ballfield with the two boys afterwards.

3: The next day at school, Virgil is absent.

4: (which should be #2) Detail their close friendship, and love of music. His present thrill, the discovery of a 45 rpm in a box in a thrift shop: Stan Kenton's orchestra with June Christy

64

singing *Across the Alley from the Alamo*. Brenda had given him a trumpet for his 16th birthday. He began taking lessons. It wasn't long before he was good. Very good. Details. The day he was absent from school, after the evening she had spent with the boys, she telephoned Virgil's mom, who said he hadn't come down for breakfast (Brenda having phoned from school), but being moody, nothing unnatural for Virgil to not come down for breakfast. Would she go up and check his room? Yes. His mom goes up. Virgil's not there. Finds a note on his pillow: *Dear Mother, I'll be seeing you. Love, Kid Stuff.*

Virgil's mom, just like Brenda's parents, had taken each other's child as part of the family, accustomed to Virgil and Brenda playing records, writing scripts for puppet plays, making and painting the puppets, as well as the clothes, even the music, for productions on certain Sunday afternoons, for neighborhood entertainment. Doing homework together. Going to movies, concerts, plays. Devoted friends. But when Virgil's mom told Brenda Virgil took his trumpet with him, it was as clear as dawn over the Rockies that the novelist had not only the end of his novel, but the last line.

5: The two ballplayers say farewell to each other, after the last day of school. Their families have money, the boys have it easy. But they're good kids, the one more superficial and material minded than the other, yet each, in secret, has a certain greed for pleasures of the body. Give a little background with examples. Low key.

Both boys leave for summer vacations to different places, returning in the fall to go away to different colleges, where each meets and becomes engaged to a young woman, and after graduation, gets married, has kids and a nine-to-five. Here's a change. The man who played shortstop in high school, with his wife expecting their second child, faints at his desk in the ad agency where he works. He's taken to the hospital where he goes into coma and dies that night.

The second baseman, married with kids, runs for office, makes a name for himself, pretty much a young, and then middle-aged politician in the news: the day Brenda sees him in the lounge at O'Hare he's being tracked by cameras and reporters. In a three piece suit, hair silver, has a tan, teeth as white as snow. Brenda's hair is short, and in curls, streaked with grey, not the long auburn hair and bangs of highschool, and her mature body, still lean, her breasts low and full, dark eyes more piercing than ever, and her pretty face not a mask to hide wild emotions, but open, wise, and of experience. Belted dark green jacket, white dress, good legs, worn, tan ankle high boots. As she watches the politician preen, her heart hardens, in bitterness. As a figure, in the crowd, she stands out.

He sees her.

She smiles and gestures that he continue — the interview — but! His eyes widen! Face turns scarlet, quick! Turns away from the cameras, whips out a hanky, fakes a false sneeze, cameras lower, everybody waits. He gathers himself, makes apologies, glances at Brenda, the reporters follow his gaze, but Brenda is gone. His relief is visible, he laughs, eyes twinkling. What a sneeze *that* was! Amusement.

Something about Bren's visiting her grandchildren, daughter's kids. Illness, background, some detail.

Bren has kept in touch with Virgil's mother, who, it will appear, has every once in a while heard from Virgil, but never mentioned it to Bren because she assumed he was in touch with Bren as well. Maybe bring this in, no, have it follow the scene, where Bren, while standing in line at the counter of the record store, in the city where her daughter lives, to buy as a gift, the newest record by The Mirrors. As she waits in line, she looks around. Sees a section of new Japanese imports, and there, on the cover of one, a photo of Virgil, playing his trumpet, and behind him, his band: the name, on the side of the bass drum: *The Eager Beaver*.

She buys that record, too, and after the visit to her daughter, visits Virgil's mom. Give geo location and background details. Tells his mom the story. All of it, from the beginning.

"I see," his mom says. "Are you happy in your life?"

"I was. But I'm not." Pause. "I have had everything anyone could want. Yet," she lowered her eyes, "in a way that's not enough. Something," looked at the other woman, "died in me when Virgil left."

"Well," Virgil's mom sighed, "it died in me, too. Maybe I shouldn't say this, but Virgil loved you more than you knew, and it wasn't kid stuff. That's why he called himself Kid Stuff. Why don't you go see him?"

"*See* him?"

"Sure! You've got the money."

"Where is he?"

"Japan!"

Brenda's farewell to her husband. Whom she likes and does not. She's divided. Anyway she goes. Flies to Japan. And the end of the novel.

Chapter Three: *Eager Beaver*

BUT NO. Decided to outline with detail, the action at the ballgame, as well as afterward, as she walks toward the parking lot with the two boys, leaving Virgil behind.

He wrote in pencil above the first line on a yellow legal pad: THE BALLGAME:

In the top of the fourth inning they turned over a double play: 6-4-3: short to second to first. Two down. But the throw from second to first missed the runner's right eye by a whisker, and the runner, angry, swung at the second baseman who ducked. The shortstop, being right there, smacked the runner. The runner bounced back, and again swung at the second baseman who jumped backwards, out of reach. The shortstop moved in, saying something to the runner, which the right fielder, who had come in to back up, thought he heard the short-stop say, "Don't you *touch* him!" Knowing they were close friends, although the second baseman had tears in his eyes, no one knew if they were from gratitude, excitement, or fear (fear), while the short-stop and runner swung at each other, and both teams rushed in — bam bam bam: the game continues. Our team wins. Brenda and Virgil, watching from the bench near third base, ecstatic. Brenda herself near tears because of the shortstop's declaration (she didn't need to hear what he said: fighting for his second baseman).

Describe Virgil and Brenda keeping score. Virgil's antics. And — anyway, after the game, Brenda, so overcome by the shortstop's bravado, she — with Virgil — waits for them, until they come out of the locker room, in slacks and shirts. She flings her arms around the shortstop's neck, kisses his cheek —

"I love you! *Love* you!"

Both boys embarrassed, and puzzled. She pleads —

"May I come with you?"

They looked, go into narrative past tense, they looked at Virgil, and at each other. Virgil, who hadn't expected this, was startled, and it showed. But Brenda didn't see it because she was seeing nothing but being with them, and doing with them, what they did with each other, in her infra-red binoculars, her passion. Breathing fast:

"Aw, *Hey*! Come *on*!"

Used to getting her way.

"Sure," the shortstop grinned, and linking arms with them, they walked toward the shortstop's dark blue convertible, Brenda unaware of Virgil. Who stood on the cement area outside the locker room, deserted ballfield behind him, watching, with a dark hurt Brenda had never seen. She waved over her shoulder to Virgil, grinned to the guys, and piped:

"See ya later!"

Happy laughter.

"What are you talking about?"

"You. *You* know."

"We do *not* know!"

"No. We don't. Honest."

"I won't tell anybody. I haven't yet, have I? I'm the only one who knows, and *I won't tell*!"

"Tell what?"

"I saw you guys come out of the bathroom, and—"

"And what?"

"Brenda, what *is* it?"

"Let me do it with you! *Please*!"

"Do what?"

"Aw, hey. Come on. Just because I'm a girl, I can do those things, too!" Pause. "You know." Eyes heavy lidded. "Want me to show you?"

They looked at each other, and shook their heads. No idea what she was talking about.

Thus Brenda went home frustrated, body set in a seething fury, excreting juices, went as through a wringer, leaving her exhausted. Yet as body began the slow return to normal, her mind began to function, and she realized she was stuck in a story nobody would believe. The thought of Virgil, the Prince of Hearts, filled her with such remorse, she felt trapped in a certainty she didn't understand, for her hungry body had taken control, and her abandonment and seeming betrayal of Virgil, in terms of what followed with those infielders, influenced her choice of husband, and in part explained her lifelong duty, and devotion, to him and her family.

But the next day, her emotions still trapped, on realizing Virgil hadn't come to school (without her knowing why was impossible, it had never happened), she was also trapped in the outer world of someone else. A sad, sorry, and tender location.

Phoned Virgil's mother.

Flashback to Virgil and Bren in his room, at home, playing records. Stan Kenton's *Eager Beaver*. They scat to it. Bren's brief dialogue (to establish closeness) with his mom, before she goes home.

The boys say farewell to each other. This scene has a finality to it that serves, in tone, as predictive.

"How did she *know*?"

"Will you keep in touch?"

"No. This—is it. If Mary Lynne ever found out, it would be death."

"So it's goodbye. Just plain goodbye. For ever."

"I'm too afraid. Yes."

"But you liked it." Pause. "You said so."

He held out his hand, but the other drew away. Sitting on a low hill, under trees, at night. By the railroad tracks. A quarter moon hung in a starless sky, above warehouses, beyond which the dark skyline of the city.

"I did like it. I do like it, but it isn't all there is!" Trying to convince himself. "What will *you* do?"

"Go to college, like you, and, like you, get married and have kids. As to other men, I don't know. It scares me, too, but we've had so much fun. It's been so good. I'm not going to be happy without you." In darkness, his eyes were sad. He sighed, too fearful to say it, too self-conscious to know how . . .

"Living won't be the same."

"That was crazy of you to smack that runner. But thanks."

"Your throw almost took his ear off—"

"No! Don't *kiss* me!"

"Okay. That was crazy of you to show up at Diane's party, dressed like a girl. Remember my kiss? Was that crazy?"

They smiled.

"Yes. It was crazy. All. Me, dancing with Dracula, you biting my neck, everybody in hysterics. I was so embarrassed . . ."

"I was too, but I was *Dracula*!"

"My mother helped me dress, and she couldn't stop laughing. 'You're so *cute!*' she kept saying. Did you know that?"

"No, but she was right."

"Oh well. I have to go."

"I know. Me too. I'll miss you."

The other was silent. They rose, wiped dust from their jeans, walked down the hill, and arms out walked on the shining, moonlit, steel tracks—to an asphalt road, where they stepped off and turned to walk home.

"Did I tell you what Virgil Eager said to me, the day after the party?"

"No." Pause. "He's a creep."

"He was in love with Brenda. Did you know that?"

"I don't care. My parents can't stand him, and are disgusted with Brenda's folks for letting her see so much of him."

"I know. Did you see his face, that day she came home with us?"

"No, I didn't see anything. I wanted to get away from her. She scared hell out of me! How did she *know*!"

"I don't know, and I've often wondered . . . her house right across the street . . . but she hasn't told anybody." Pause. "No. She wouldn't."

"Why?"

"She's too honest. I can't figure her out. She's smart, real smart. People like her. But there's more to it, she's kind of complicated. I like her."

"You do?"

"Yes. Poor Virgil. Brenda's heartbroken. I wonder where he is."

"To hell with him."

"Want to hear what he said, about you and me?"

"Go on, tell me."

Revealing an irritation. The other paused before he spoke, because they were at the beginning of the driveway, that separated their houses.

"Well, what *was* it!"

"He said: 'Dracula at shortstop, and Snow White at second. A romantic combination, don't you think?' "

"What did you say?"

"I didn't say anything. I thought it was funny. I laughed."

"And Virgil?"

"He thought it was funny, too. And he laughed. He was right, and he knew it, that's why we laughed—"

The second baseman slapped him on the arm, said,

"Take care of yourself," and walked toward the front door of his house: crisp white door set in clean red brick between tall pine bushes, facing an emerald lawn. Just that clear his words were a lie, from the lips of a high-school boy who imagined he would be a man, to walk way out there, in his life ahead, from one woman to another, conquest to conquest, leaving memories behind like clouded mirrors, hazy reflections, and wonder why something was missing.

"Goodbye!" Shortstop called.

Out loud, startling him, for it seemed to echo. He was angry. His body was hungry, and his heart was hurt. Without knowing why, he turned, and looked across the street, at Brenda's house. The light in her room was on. So, she was home.

What was she doing tonight?

Today. Last day of school. She was very different, quiet, too quiet, and too much alone, since Virgil ran away, and Dracula was sad. For himself, for Brenda, and for Virgil, wherever Virgil was, and, in a way he couldn't yet understand, for Snow White, too.

A note on the kitchen table said *Call Diane*.

He called Diane.

"Where have you been?" Peeved. He saw her face before him. Said he'd been out for a walk, with (Shortstop). Did she want him to come over?

"Yes." Read off a brief list of food he should bring. He took notes. Would be right over.

Surprise party.

As he backed his convertible into the street, shifted and drove westward to the supermarket, in his rear view mirror he saw that the light in Brenda's room was out. Her small house, set back among trees, deep in shadows, seemed itself to speak, low, in a whisper: *goodbye.*

With Virgil's 16th birthday coming up, Brenda had been frantic. What to *give* him?

Her mom and dad, who argued, quarreled, and complained day and night anyway, were impossible. Brenda was desperate.

"Daddy! Help me!"

At the supper table.

"He's a nice boy," her father said. Brenda knew what was coming: "a little weird, but —"

"Don't say that, George! He's Bren's *best friend*!"

"Bren knows what I think."

"But don't *say* it!"

"*You* do!"

"STOP IT!" Brenda cried. Burst into tears.

Both her parents looked at each other, in silent, superior wisdom, before their heads turned to look at Brenda, with concern.

"He likes music," her dad said. "I saw an ad for trumpets, on sale, down at Albert Pittis's."

Brenda's mom raised her eyebrows, and her eyes grew large as she smiled from ear to ear.

Brenda, who resembled her mom, did the same, and on her

youthful face, the transition from tears and a gloomy scowl to a happy smile was so rapid her dad chuckled . . .

So, the next day after school, as it began to snow, Brenda went to Albert Pittis's, and with the hundred dollars her dad (grumpy) had given her, which she *promised* PROMISED to pay back, and with money of her own, she bought a brand new Conn, a student trumpet, for a hundred and eighty-five . . .

Gold with silver fittings, in a black case, compartments lined with dark blue velvet. On the left side, the horn itself. On the right, in smaller indentations: a small jar of valve oil, a soft square of cloth — to polish — and in the last, in a small cloth sleeve with a flap, its inside softer than the polishing cloth, the silver mouthpiece.

Closed, latched, and gift-wrapped.

"Don't have a heart attack," her dad told her, the morning of Virgil's birthday, "you're too young."

"Oh be still," her mom said.

"What did I say?" asked her father.

"I'm so excited I can't think," Brenda said. "I can't *wait* until he sees it! You know, the music teacher told our class if you can whistle a melody, that's the first step to playing it, on any instrument, because it's in your mind, and ear, and Virgil can whistle *anything!*"

"That's true," dad agreed, repeating: "That's true."

"He sings, too," mom smiled. "Has a *good* voice!"

"That's also true."

"You."

"So there!" Brenda cried, face flushed: her intuition filled her awareness. She *knew* he'd love it. *Knew* it!

That night in Virgil's living room, his mom served cookies and milk. Sat on the rug, in front of a fire, a warm, shaded glow from corner lamps, Virgil anxious, too, and preferred a softer light, as he opened presents from his mom: *The Daring Young Man on the Flying Trapeze and Other Stories,* by William Saroyan. Two Punch and Judy punk rock hand puppets in funny dresses, and a tape of selections from the Abbott and Costello show. Brenda very impressed by these gifts, oh yes, for Virgil was delighted by them — and while they listened to those funny radio comedians: "Who's on second! What's on first!" Virgil and Brenda, with the hand puppets, acted out in mime, the dialogue of the show, in hysterics, as Brenda imitated her parents quibbling as well, causing her a little guilt, being so involved in a gift for someone else was selfish, Virgil clicked off the tape machine, and looked at Brenda, who lowered her eyes.

"What's the matter?" he asked.

"She's worn out," Virgil's mom smiled, touching his knee,

72

"from knowing what's in that package for you."

Brenda nodded, trying to veil her eyes, keeping her face a mask—

Virgil used his fingers as tiny puppets to push and angle the gift toward him, opened the envelope, read the birthday card, undid the yellow ribbon in miniature ballet motions, and unwrapped the deep green glossy paper as if TOP SECRET, placed it to one side, crossed his legs Indian fashion, lifted the case onto his lap, slid the latches with his thumbs, raised the lid of the case, and saw, twinkling in firelight, his golden trumpet, nestled in deep blue velvet.

"Happy birthday Virgil," Brenda said. Her vision blurred.

"Thank you," he replied, but it came out a whisper, he swallowed, and again. He glanced at his mom.

"Boy oh boy," she said. "Take it out," she said. "Let's see how it works."

Virgil lifted the trumpet from velvet, removed the small, soft, little bag with a flap which he raised, and removed the silver mouthpiece, which he inserted into the horn, as his left hand held the valve-casings, and his right index fingertip, second and third fingertips rested on the mother-of-pearl keys. He drew the mouthpiece to his lips, pressed them against the warm metal, his head lowered somewhat, not wanting to be pretentious, he breathed into the horn, fingertips soft on the keys.

The two women or—his mom and Brenda—watched, spellbound. Brenda, lips parted, just about to speak, changed her mind. And it hurt not to say it.

As water is to earth, and the moon to tides, her realization of the relation of that trumpet to that boy: his rosebud lips were created for that mouthpiece, and his long, slender, artistic fingers seemed extensions of the keys, thus he was of music, to music. For music. *In music, with music.*

By firelight.

At his mother's side.

Brenda bit her lip.

Item: Virgil detests Snow White, while Brenda, although impressed by Virgil's seriousness, says she "loves him! Those double plays! And he can *hit*!"

"Singles," Virgil sneered. "If he hits into left, the runner on second can't score. I *loathe* him. He's like his father: handsome, superficial and selfish, they're two of a kind. Capitalist swine in a pretty little American suburb. Did you know his parents voted No for aid

73

to education for minority groups, and Yes for city funds for private schools? Filthy racists!"

But Brenda didn't want to hear that, although it was true, for her body had truths of its own, and as regards Dracula and Snow White, she yearned for them both at once in a sexual blur, and a hidden dream they'd merge into one. Looking through her infra-red binoculars those nights, body cried for eruption.

Okay.

After Virgil runs away, Bren, as best she can for obvious reasons (guilt for what she had done. For what she had done without thinking of him. For her anger at his running away, and in fear that he might not return), took care of his mom as he had done and would have done: through letters, phone calls, cards, and visits, while home from college. After Bren is engaged (figure out a Nice Guy who accepts her as she is—with all that guilt—happy to do so, for in secret he thinks he's a loser)—Virgil's mom rents Virgil's room to a woman her own age. They become fast friends, have a lot in common. Bren graduates from college, gets married, and—pregnant and house hunting, her contact with Virgil's mom tapers off, but she phones her, and tells her why, that she'll be in touch as soon as she's settled. Virgil's mom soothes Brenda, etc., but again, doesn't mention that Virgil has begun to send money home, in letters from all sorts of places, here, and in Europe, on occasion with photos, always ending by saying he prays for her, and will always love her. With no return address. He's always on the move. She doesn't mention this to Bren thinking he's written her the same, yet not altogether for that reason, realizing after long consideration, Virgil had run away from Brenda, and better let that be.

Bring into focus his high school trumpet lessons, private teacher, descriptions, character sketch of teacher. Virgil memorized big band trumpet solos, from 78 and 33⅓ rpm records, using a mute so as not to blast the neighborhood. Carried his mouthpiece wherever he went, played it as an instrument of its own. Did drum solos—hand and finger—on tabletops, or parked cars, whistling a tune, from memorized sheet music, or on tapes, his records, radio, or in his head. Albert Pittis, the owner and manager of the store, got to know Virgil, one day let him borrow a tape of Michel André playing Albinoni's Trumpet Concerto, Virgil was hooked, and off he sailed into classical European music.

Note:
The passage where Bren sees what the adult politician Snow White

has become, in the O'Hare airline terminal lounge — This is off. Give it more impact.

In his hotel suite that evening, while changing for supper, the politician finds a note in the left front pocket of his trousers. He takes it along with change, from the pocket, separates and unfolds it, to read a strong feminine script, the words: *The most human thing you ever did was to let Dracula love you. The rest is fake and hypocrisy.*

World famous trembled in his stocking feet. Perspiration appeared on his brow. Mouth dry. What ran through his mind — how did the note get in his pocket? Who put it there? Did *she* write it? Yes! Who else? — came as threats that equalled the note itself, so assuming Brenda wrote it, he couldn't stop thinking: *How did she know?* and felt an icy chill, deep in his guts, shimmer down into his bowels, as he remembered, from yesteryear: *"How did she know?"* feeling Shortstop's body in a thunderbolt of passion: his vision blurred, he felt weak, sat on the edge of the bed, and looked around.

He burned the note in an ashtray.

Nothing he could do. Nothing. Nothing. So. He went on with his tour, each day, as nothing, as if nothing had taken place in his past with Brenda, or her note. His confidence returned, and he went on getting votes, respected throughout the dry, plastic mold of midwestern America: conservative without color or creativity. The past was a dream best forgotten, until, of course, in bed with his wife, or another woman, as the weeks became months, it entered his mind, while making love, that he'd lied to himself, which is why his orgasms hurt so, because he wanted that beautiful body of that beautiful boy, who had loved him. It became so obsessive he searched all over her body for him, and kissing her, one night he called her a name which puzzled her. Later that night, he spoke in his sleep, alas, for what he said was no puzzle at all.

Would he see a shrink?

No. Too frightened, and too

Unconscious. Yeah. Maybe his wife tells him, or suggests it: "You said something in your sleep, last night, dear, and—"

Would he ask her what it was?

Or would he know and be too afraid?

Wait. At this point in his career, he's at the top of national security. Everything he says, does, wherever he goes, whoever he sees, involves national security.

Right. If he saw a shrink, there'd be questions.

If it leaked —
He'd kill himself.
Okay. He's distraught. Everybody knows he fucks around, but —
He's got to talk to somebody.
Good. Who?
Brenda?
(Amusement) That'd be fun! Can't you see it? But no. Let's hang him.
Think.

After Brenda's JAL Flight 425 arrived in Tokyo, and while in line going through customs, she noticed the beginning of a column on the front page of *The Washington Post,* which was folded in half, on top of a briefcase, resting on top of luggage belonging to the businessman in line in front of her. The column read, to the fold —

> It was rumored during Monday's White House breakfast [Snow White], the President's closest advisor and personal courier to the Pentagon, said, in apparent surprise, "My God, sir! I never noticed it! But . . ." *gulp* "You look like *Dracula*!" Burst into laughter, and collapsed.
>
> The cause of his remark is unknown, and while [Snow White] undergoes treatment in the Psychiatric Division at Walter Reed Hospital, experts are baffled . . .

Well, no wonder, Brenda thought, recalling one evening after the encounter, watching the news, to see Snow White standing next to the President, Congressmen and bodyguards on the steps of the Lincoln Monument, everybody all smiles, the President looked a LOT like Shortstop!

Snow White recovered enough to be released from the hospital, held a press conference, said he had been unable to sleep because of his concern over international terrorism and U.S. security, and the sleeping tablet his doctor prescribed had had an adverse effect, causing him to see in the President a likeness to a close childhood friend (mention the double-play combo), who passed away long ago. Snow White held up a glossy of Dracula, camera went in for a close up, sure enough, there he was.

So Snow White and his wife went on a vacation, to fish, swim and outline plans for heightened national security. One night, a week later, in their cabin by the lake, surrounded by FBI agents hidden behind bushes, in trees, and on the roof, while his wife slept, Snow White tip-toed into the den, and took the same vacation Hemingway took, the permanent kind, and, in his craziness, to get to Dracula

76

as fast as possible, like Ernest, Snow White used a shotgun: against the roof of his mouth, too.

Mt. Fuji was a dark and rising stage prop with a bright white cap on top, under a painted starry sky.

Brenda got out of the taxi, paid and tipped the driver, and turned to gaze at the roadhouse, as the cab sped onto the highway, gathered speed, and vanished in the oriental night.

From the front door, to where she stood, even beyond where she stood, Japanese cars, scooters and bikes of all description fanned out, something to see, for the parking lot was large.

The air was clear and cool, and against the dark hills which led to Fuji, the big band music from within the building was as clear and keen as the neon sign on its side, as high as the wall, a tall one-storey: within a large, deep yellow circle, a bright green vertical eighth note served as background for brilliant, deep blue script on a slant to divide the circle in half: *The Eager Beaver,* in English and Japanese.

As she made her way between cars to the front door, she heard muted cheers and applause. She reached the door, solid wood, took one step up, it opened to her touch. Before she stepped forward, however, she paused, in thought. Turned, gazed at the parking lot, and racing headlights of busy traffic, on the highway. She stepped inside, the door closed behind her. A light went on. A Japanese man sat at a table, face half hidden by a hanging lampshade, his hands opening the lid of a metal cashbox, he smiled, accepting the equivalent in yen of a U.S. ten:

"Welcome to the Beaver. The joint is jammed, you might try for a spot at the bar, on your right," he gestured. "To dig the sounds, and catch the scene."

"Thanks," she smiled.

The fellow rose, stepped to his left and parted dark blue velvet drapes, indicating the three carpeted steps leading up, into the club, and as she went up the steps, the man watched her, and thought: *Who is she?*

And at the top of the steps the scene stopped her cold, catching her breath. She'd never seen anything like it.

The building, in fact of cinderblock, coated with cement and painted a dark gray, during the day looked like a warehouse. But the interior was stunning. The ceiling was a low dome, covered with black velvet, tiny mirrors sparkling, like stars. The floor plan almost circular with the bandstand opposite the front door, and at eye level. From where she stood, the floor leading to the bandstand was on a low descent, and filled with tables and chairs and all kinds of people,

77

eating and drinking and talking. Excitement in the air. Handsome young men and pretty young women waited tables, rushing to and from the kitchen. A sophisticated air-conditioning system drew smoke from the place, thus the air was clear.

To her left, hatcheck room. To her right, a long bar doing a swell business, keeping four bartenders busy, in their sparkling white shirts, red vests, before blue-mirrored rows of bottles, sending slivers of light, winking, all a-sparkle as couples and friends stood three deep, behind seated customers.

Beyond the hatcheck room, an exit, beyond which the kitchen next to a sushi bar. Another exit. The bandstand. Another exit, and a roped-off VIP-seeming area, at present jammed with Japanese teenagers. Beside the far end of the liquor bar.

The multi-racial educated and attractive crowd was dazzling with culture. Table after table, eager faces in candle glow, in the soft, pale peach color of the air, for the walls were rose, tablecloths white, and candlelit faces and shining eyes caused an overall color of air to reflect the stimulus in the event, for the event was music. The brass railing around the dining area seemed to glow, in the way those people created a glow, like a low fire, beneath a black sky, and sparkling stars.

The band was of course on the bandstand, and according to section, in tiers, with the trumpets—four, on the top, beside the triangle, and bassoon. Five trombones on the next tier down, next to six saxophones (two alto, two tenor, two soprano) beside the clarinet. Next down, electric guitar, flute, and instruments she couldn't identify, with, at stage level, and center, a Steinway piano facing a single violin. On the far upperleft, the drums, and on the side of the bass drum facing the audience, to match the neon sign outside, white letters outlined with glitter on black, said: *The Eager Beaver*. At stage center, in animated and amusing conversation with the Japanese violinist, a teenage girl, was Virgil Eager himself, his trumpet in his left hand at his side as he talked, and members of the band listened, amused. A band as diverse as the audience. And all the people talking and enjoying the action, every one of them, aware of the imminent entrance of music, for no matter where they sat or stood in the dining area or at the bar, and no matter who was saying what to whom, sidelong glances never lost sight of that man, at the center of the stage, with his trumpet in hand at his side. Therefore, as he raised his trumpet, his nervousness part of his charm, and played a few notes as if part of the dialogue, the girl raised her violin, she too played a few notes, and it was in that affectionate way that they both approached the microphone, the Japanese teenagers in the VIP area began to cheer and whistle and carry on, Brenda realized the violinist was why they came. Seeing

Virgil there, up there, in a dark blue single-breasted suit, white shirt open at the collar, her heart melted, and she yearned to speak with him, so without knowing what she was doing, being drawn to him, she began walking toward the stage.

"What did you think of that last number?" Virgil asked the audience.

Whistles, applause, cheers.

"How about a little *Flapjack?*"

And stepped back with a smile, the club fell silent, hushed. Waiters froze, bartenders too. Brenda kept walking.

Looking great, curly auburn hair streaked with gray, classic, diamond earrings, white dress, mandarin collar, sheer silk stockings and black and white spectator pumps, she seemed to float, she felt she was floating. Virgil saw her as he raised his trumpet. He lowered it. Held up a hand to the band, and crossed to her. He knelt down. She looked up.

"Bren," he said. Could say no more.

"I came to see you. I've missed you."

"Bren," he said, "you don't understand . . ." and she saw his face, up close, was vague, and his eyesockets hollow, skin rather gray, was he on drugs? He held up a hand, as if in apology, returned to center stage, and the mike. But before he raised his trumpet, she heard a low tattoo on snare drums, followed by brushes. She looked up. Jo Jones, with his wise eyes, gazed down on her, his expression sad, and all-comprehending, all-knowing, she almost staggered backwards, brought her hand to her parted lips, green eyes wide: *Jo Jones was dead!*

Virgil was watching her, his eyes haunted, and sad, oh *so sad,* with the slightest motion he lowered his eyes, shook his head, faced the audience, raised his trumpet and hit C above high C with a hard, open horn, his phrasing hard and even, short snaps: one two three four beat *bam, bam, bam, bam* while the violinist doubled Virgil's rhythm, in crisp notes, *The Camptown Races,* as the introduction to *Flapjack,* Jo Jones coming in on a roll. The piano player chorded with his left hand, and right hand in counterpoint to the violin as the trumpet and trombone sections rose, all horns muted, and in unison played it like a dirge, with the violin dancing around Virgil's trumpet, and Jo Jones' brushes in the background, like snowfall, the scene dimmed, blurred, she felt herself rise, on an invisible rising wave as the saxophones came in, up beat for a fox trot, toward the sunrise, but the closer she got the sun seemed farther away, behind a hill or cloud, and it was in an odd light of dawn that Virgil dropped two octaves and the tenor saxophone took his solo, she found herself behind the wheel of a rented car. Parked in front of a house in New England.

A house next door to a Burger King. But behind, back in the rear of the property. The grass was matted and dry. The house vacant. Closed and locked. A plastic sign in the yard: FOR SALE. The violin jumped two octaves, and held, playing Virgil's former one, two, three, four, beat, and Virgil's trumpet danced around her, in the orchestrated reversal. The house where Virgil's mother lived.

Brenda cut the engine, opened the door, got out, closed the door, and walked across the cold yard, in late March. Ground still frozen, the wind had a bite. She rubbed her hands, cold in her evening dress, she made her way with care, for high heels were not the thing. But up the front steps, across the small porch, she looked inside, through the front door window, to see little left but dust. All furniture gone, nothing there at all, in emptiness and chill, save hidden tiny spiders, and a feel of death.

Yet as if it had appeared there, in the doorway from the hallway to the kitchen in the back, she saw an envelope. But the front door was locked. So, down the steps in an alto saxophone solo she went around to the back, following a narrow cement walk, hearing a dog bark. The dog was not near, nor far, and up two steps to the back door, which on her touch swung open, inward, she saw the envelope. Crossed the floor. Picked it up. The door swung closed. And she opened the letter as the sun came out, warming the entire landscape to a bass violin being bowed, slow, with Brenda reading handwriting in blue but faded blue, ball point ink, paper musty, *I'll be seeing you. Love, Kid Stuff* becoming an illustrated comic strip from a daily paper. In the first frame the wreck of a car, driver's door open, driver dead. A trumpet beside his left foot. In the second frame, his mother being evicted by a fat man in a suit, and in the third frame, which extended into the fourth, their gravestones together, in a mound of mud. Two crosses, none of the markings clear, set on an angle at the foot of a twisted, solitary leafless tree against a dark and stormy sky, the band fell still, save a classical violin solo backed up by the same on trumpet, backed up the same by bassoon. Clouds began to boil, the wind gathered force, Jo picked up his sticks and the sun went down. The sky seemed to thrash in the sound of a low growl with a scream in the center, the whole band began to open up, first by solos, next by sections and in the end, all together it began to snow. Up tempo. She ran down the street where she lived, clarinet and winds, opened the front door and ran down the hall, turned, brass sections wide open, raced upstairs in a hard, driving staccato of sticks on snaredrum, fled down the hall to her room, flung open the door, ran in and, sticks on cymbals, hard and fast: *bamba, bamba, bamba, bamba* leaped onto her bed in a crash of all drums, crescendo blast, full band, in weaving sheets of sound, Brenda woke up, in silence, on the floor beside her bed, near to the open window, infra-red binoculars in hand, fading wild applause, cheers, whistles, and general pandemonium, to eventual silence, deep in shadow, long in echo. She crawled to the window, so scared she couldn't breathe, she raised the binoculars, found the range and focus, on the room in the house across the street. But the room was empty, and the house was dark, as in a dream.

He finished setting the small rosewood table, making sure the candlewicks were upright so she could light them without a fuss, and after folding the evening paper, and arranging it with her mail—to the left of the round, blue and green, floral cotton placemat: first class mail on top, second—first class mail on top of second class mail: she got a lot of mail (being an active person in politics, outspoken in local causes, plus the mail from her three children away in college, the best, you understand, the best schools in the country): he went in the kitchen and double-checked the fridge: lamb chops in aluminum foil, broccoli ends sautéed in olive oil and garlic, the small bottle of chilled white wine, returned the way he had come, took the elevator to the third floor, walked down the carpeted hallway, and went into his room.

She would never understand, he knew, and it was with, it was in that certainty that he sat at his desk, which—his desk faced an open window with a view of the long, green yard with pine trees and rose gardens sloping off toward the desert and nothing but sky beyond: it was with a heavy heart that he wrote her his note of farewell. This was the best job he'd ever had.

So it was in a scent of roses that he rolled a piece of orange paper into his yellow Olivetti portable typewriter, with a blue ribbon. He typed:

Dear Madame:

It is with considerable regret that I write this note. I have enjoyed my stay here as I have none other.

It has been an honor to serve you. But in view of the event last night, as I helped your friend Mar Vel to the door, I can no longer stay in this house.

She'll never understand, he thought.
But wrote:

On arriving at my destination I shall write you a note giving an address where I may be reached. I would be grateful if you would forward my wages to date, with a letter of recommendation.

(signature)
Your Gentleman Manservant

He folded the paper, put it in a lavender envelope, sealed it, wrote her name on the front, rose from his desk and in a depressed frame of mind packed his things: he travelled light, a large cloth bag with handle loops in an orange, blue and black paisley design held all. He looked round his room. Bed made, window open a crack, neat job, he left, closed the door behind him, walked down the hall, stepped

82

into the elevator, and descended to the main floor, stepped out—onto the long Oriental rug, along which he walked, turned left into the living room, and dining room, placed the envelope on her dinner plate, walked to the front door, and, just as Mar Vel had, he opened it, stepped outside, closed it, heard the lock click shut, he dropped the key in the mail slot which opened inside the house, and moved down the curving flagstone walk passing beautiful gardens: rose red on grass green beneath pine trees, set against distant hills, the air fresh, and filled with scent, he stood on the last flagstone, making sure the electric eye would trigger a faraway bell, he counted to ten, and stepped onto sand.

He walked out into the desert, and onward, toward the horizon. She had fainted in his arms as Mar Vel said farewell, and, he realized, by her hot breath on his ear, as she kissed him, that it was not Mar Vel, it was *him*! but why, he wondered, in that way? realizing (as he walked), it was in just that exact way, she let Mar Vel know, yet—his steps were brisk across flat, dry sand—after, she had touched him, felt how hot he was, and fainted, or pretended to, how was he to know? she whispered *you, you, burn me,* Mar Vel was gone, the door was closed, he held her in his arms, her breath came fast, heart pounding. He lifted her, held her small, slight body in both arms, took her to her room on the second floor, arranged her on her bed for she was asleep she was no not asleep she was between: he drew the beautiful afghan blanket from the foot of her bed up over her body, tucked it around her shoulders, and under her chin raising her head to slide the pillow in a silver glitter in the deep blue sky signalled, he prayed, the arrival of the plane, which proved to be the case, yes, the twin engine Lockheed Elektra circled above him, dipped wings, banked and came in on a fine smooth landing, for the desert surface was hard, the plane stopped, and as propellor blades idled a door opened in the side of the plane, a small aluminum ladder appeared followed by a woman who hopped from one rung onto sand, and walked toward him, as he began to run, to her, his cloth bag in hand.

She was tall, slender and tan, with choppy light brown hair, blue eyes, white teeth, they embraced, kissed, and arm in arm returned to the silver ship.

"Will she understand?" she asked.

"No," he said, offering to help her on board, she needed none, was inside in a wink, her hand outstretched, which he took, and thus entered the plane. She lifted the ladder in, closed and locked the door. They walked, in a stoop, to the cockpit and he realized she smelled of jasmine, and he tasted apples: Mutsu.

He sat in the co-pilot's seat beside her as she gunned the engines, the plane taxied across sand, rose deep into the blue like a dream, and at 17,000 feet, thinking of the sleeping woman, he held hands with the pilot.

He gazed down on the table, at the blue application form, fiddled with a green Bic and, thinking to end the story in the way of beginning one, or another, he filled in the blanks, writing name and address he had no address, so the completed form read that his address was the location of the place where this writing was being written: in the top chamber of the north westernmost turret of the castle overlooking the ocean.

Duration of his occupation? Life. References? Ghost, and Hand. Address? As Above. Sex, boxes to be Xd in, read as follows: Male Female Other Both. He chose the last two, in the sudden smell of garlic and sesame oil, stir-fried with shrimp and scallions, bok choy, red peppers, and fresh lime juice.

A window was above the table, on which appeared a finished manuscript and a pair of reading glasses beside a slender vase of daffodils. The window arced at top and was of leaded squares of stained glass, each square with a motif of monks, or nuns, at prayer, in rich colors which, he realized was a casement window, so he reached across, put his hand on the knob, turned and watched as it cranked open until it stopped. Stuck.

But he saw the ocean and smelled the brine in the sound of remote flying creatures he saw cloud forms appear — perhaps, because from his great height — he saw, in black and white, long arms with fists gripping lids of garbage cans as if shields in battle, also holding small wooden swords in a swirl of old boots, ladders, junk and trash within the sphere, as if a floating planet, a puffy cloud high above the horizon line of the ocean, and the crash of the surf below, in the sky.

Who Was Ted?

—for Alice Notley

HOME! Christmas vacation—first year of college, see mom and dad and sis, get together with pals back from other schools, although in secret he imagined it dull, after the excitement of being away . . . yet the closer he got, in the armored limo, tooling down the barricaded corridor from the jetport, as snow began to fall, he felt light-hearted, and eager in anticipation.

*   *   *

By the middle of the 21st century things were so lopsided in terms of race, population imbalances, the female/male ratio, massive poverty and prison overcrowding, that it made sense in terms of the scale of environmental destruction: the corporate rich had taken it all, leaving parched continents with vast rivers and lakes of vinegar, and armies ever massed for war.

This situation, like a compelling guilt, created a frenzy for antiques and memorabilia from the century before: in terror of the future—would there be a future?—the past held the middle class in suspense . . .

Lobbies of colossal highrise condos called Tall Worlds, featured bulletin boards on which were pinned colorful, hand-painted signs: SALE! SALE! SALE! Apt. 22D-A, 89 FL, 1974 MICROWAVE OVEN! 1950s HULA HOOPS! BURGER KING CAPS! 1940s AUTOMATIC POP UP TOASTER! AND MORE MORE MORE! . . .

Mom had written him of grandma's death, and how she had left her "everything in the attic," so on his arrival, having cleared tele-electron/fingerprint security and photo ID, he rode up to his floor, or level, with an armed elevator operator, got off, thanked the old guy, who welcomed him home, and while watched by the fellow, the young man went down the corridor, and halting before his door, underwent further security, and as the door opened, he turned, and waved to the uniformed man in the elevator, who waved in return . . .

Entering found his Tall World home wall to wall with stuff and junk from grandma's attic, with half the people in the World there, going through it. Mom sorting, stacking, selling, while dad, perched on a padded swivel barstool, faced a mid-1960s IBM cash register, amused, pipe in corner of his mouth, peering over reading glasses, greeting friends and neighbors. Ringing up sales.

"Son!"

"Dad!" They embraced.

"What a mess!" the young man exclaimed.

"Say hi to your mother," dad smiled. "She's loving it."

Done, and after putting his bags in his room, and changing into a slacksuit, returned to the living room to help. See those magazines by the windows? He did. Separate into different piles, so he began. Sitting on the floor, a mile in the sky, beside smoked glass windows, last light of day fading beyond the smooth horizon, leaving a pale, purple twilight, dreamlike.

All kinds of magazines, large and small, a true treasure of publishing, comic books, movie magazines, *Life* and *Look, Collier's, The Saturday Evening Post,* faded copies of *The Daily Worker,* two issues of *The New Masses* . . . a piece of paper fell into his lap, which he unfolded. A piece of typewriter paper with about three paragraphs of text, double-spaced, with considerable deletions and marginal insertions, all in pencil, with a title at the top, underlined as if in afterthought, in pencil: *For Ted, on his death: July 4th, 1983.*

He read it through twice. Folded and put into pocket, ask mom and dad later, returned to his task . . . *Who was Ted?*

After everyone had gone, dad made Scotch sours, and they sat around sipping, munching chunks of pineapple as well, and doing tallies. Dazed and happy. It had been fun, and it wasn't over . . .

Dad — and mom — didn't know who Ted was, having read the message.

"I don't know who Aram is, either," dad apologized. "But whoever wrote it, wrote 'Thank you' at the end, as if for presentation, before an audience. This is a first draft, with a lot of rewriting, meaning it was done in haste, for that occasion, and given its intensity concerning poetry, it suggests Ted was a poet, and this was read to a gathering of poets, at a wake for Ted."

As a chill went up the young man's spine a high whine followed by a rapid crackling in the distance meant a laser cue rifle had located, and killed, someone with an obsolete weapon who had fired too late in return. A series of explosions with another high whine — silence, causing anxiety, for his sister was coming home, her armored limo due so soon. Every night one was hit, occupants taken hostage. No amount of barbed wire, patrolled barricades, and armed guards stopped the roving mobs of homeless poor.

Before he fell asleep that night, he re-read the message, *For Ted*

. . . thinking, the Fourth of July? Ted died on *the Fourth of July*! He must have been *some*-BODY! And the young man, weary from travel and the antique sale, fell asleep, and with a heavy heart, he had a wish. He wished he had known Ted. "My friend Ted," he would say, and to friends, "Have you met Ted?" "Ted! It's so good to see you!"

The paper fluttered from his fingers, and fell to the floor, where it rested on the carpet. His breathing softened, his sleep was deep, and in a breeze discovered himself sitting on a stone step in front of an 18th century church beside a graveyard, under an overcast, rather purple evening snowy sky, listening, as Ted, seated beside and a little above him, spoke: voice soft, yet insistent, seeming to emerge from inside the dark and empty church, in tones of a muffled drum: *boom boom boom* revealing the lost mystery of the elusive Aram . . . Ted began to appear transparent, his voice remote . . .

"TED! TED!" cried the dreamer, "TED! WAIT!"

. . . Ted, with ketchup, bits of popcorn and crumbs from potato chips, and wilted french fries down his shirt, smelling of cigarettes, fried onions and flat Pepsi, began to vanish.

"Ted, my friend," the young man wept. "Don't go."

But in the mystery of the dream, Ted departed even in that dream, thus Ted was gone forever, leaving a dark and silent church beside a graveyard, in that little neighborhood in the galaxy.

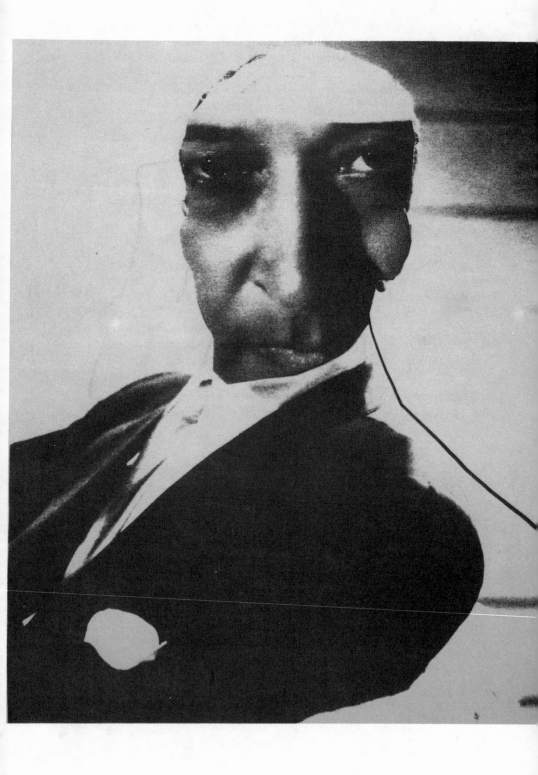

Blue

"I SAW WHITE yesterday. Downtown."

"Oh? What did he say?"

"That he'd bought some new shoes."

"That's all?"

"You know how he is, all the money in the world, material-minded, always had been. His dad a stockbroker, and mom—"

"Yes yes, of course, I know that. Did he mention me?"

"No. Should he have?"

"I don't know. Maybe not. Who knows? We used to be friends."

"Is that so?"

"Um hum. Went to grade school together."

"Hm!"

"Before he went to that private school, although even then we were close. But after he went to college, married that rich girl, and moved east—well!"

"Never saw him again. Do you think he did wrong?"

"Not at all, except that he did everything his parents told him to, and he said everything they said, often in the same tone, and if you weren't looking at him, you'd think it was them."

"*Hm!*"

"Yep. Didn't know the sound of his own voice!"

"Is that why he voted for Reagan?"

"Sure!"

Ghost

"HEY, HERB! HERB! *Great* to see you! How are you?"

"Fine. How are you?"

"Oh, you know me. Busy as ever. Grandchildren drive me nuts. Ha ha. Where are you living—still down in Pennsy?"

"No. Jersey."

"Jersey!"

"Yes. 'Fraid so."

"Well, where in Jersey?"

"Moolah."

"Moolah? You mean Mahwah."

"No. Moolah."

"Never heard of it."

"I must catch my train."

"Great seeing you! Say hello to—still married?"

"No. Goodbye. Regards to Priscilla."

"How did you know her name? Herb!—Hey, HERB!"

"Goodbye."

Footsteps.

Crowded train station.

Train whistle, fading.

Dorothy

WITH A GOLDEN TAN, in an emerald green shirt open three buttons
down, and a black bikini, black hair in long spikes, the punk look,
cute lips a natural red, little nose, teeth as white as a new baseball,
and steady, candid, dark brown eyes. Waves slipped in, licked and
tickled ankles and toes, and slid back to sea. The vast and endless
sea, under a sky so blue it seemed to transcend space: up, up, out,
out, and down to meet water and create a thin dark line stretching
left and right, as far as the eye could see.

Walking along water's edge, alone. Passing families with children
playing in the sand, and drinking soft drinks, eating hot dogs, or ice
cream. Lovers side by side: bodies soaking up sun: playing catch,
or volleyball. Walking. Chin up, lost not in thought but in the con-
sciousness that heads turned as she passed, gazes fixed on that moving supple body, so graceful. A tiny ruby in left earlobe. Delicate silver
bracelet around right ankle. Stepping along the warm, wet sand, on
the long, wide, clean, beautiful beach, in gentle breezes, under that
long, sweeping blue, blue sky.

Six large, low brick buildings faced the water from the point of
view of the highway and bus stops. Each building—half a mile apart—
had patios, tables with umbrellas, short-order food, and offered showers
and comfort stations. Behind, beyond the highway, sand dunes of
different sizes, some quite large, topped with beach grass, slanted
toward the bay, with its town, and stores, bars, cars, pets, television,
houses, boats, yards, noise, people, pollution and garbage.

A high-winged monoplane, prop driven, buzzed up from the east
toward the beach, and puttered along, some hundred feet above the
surf, towing a long waving banner ad for a local nightclub.

A man got off a crowded bus in the parking lot, and surrounded
by other bodies moved with them toward the exit gate, through which
they all went, passing the large brick building, with its busy patio,
walked onto sand.

He removed his sandals, dropped them into his shoulder bag,
and walked towards the water, looking for a space to spread his beach
towel, and apply sun tan lotion, get some rays before going swimming. He was happy: the first day of a two week vacation. He smiled
as he walked, in an expensive orange-on-red polkadot shirt with

buttondown collar, open down the front, in flow with his step, in warm breezes, around his electric blue bikini. He had a light rooftop — tar beach — tan, which would darken to a reddish tone, he'd look ten years younger . . . fingering the inch long, gold-plated safety pin clasped in the open buttonhole on the left tip of his shirt collar. Right tip buttoned down.

She saw him pause among the beach people, find a space, move into it and begin to unpack. It was, in a way, as if she recognized him. He removed his sunglasses which he tucked into shirt pocket before taking — with care — off the shirt, fold, and place it in his bag. She did a little jump seeing the glint of the pin. He spread his beach towel like a flag, terrycloth with Gauguin colors, down onto the sand. She smiled as he sat down, opened his bag, took out a small bottle of suntan oil, open it, and apply it to his ankles, and calves, working up. Just here from the city, she thought, seeing his skin color, but he had a nice face, an honest face, and a nice body. So she walked toward him, and readied her eyes to meet his.

He had focused on a Japanese family, four pairs of sandals lined up on the edge of their blanket. Mom, dad, two kids building a sand castle. She walked into his line of vision, and his eyes met hers. She approached, stood, looking down at him, he up at her, before he lowered his, as watching someone descend a ladder, she sat down beside him, eye contact sustained, crossed her legs Indian fashion, smiled, said,

"Hi. Mind if I join you?"

"Not at all," the other smiled, amused, yet rubbing his body with oil. "Didn't we meet at Dorothy's?"

"My dear," replied the other man, for he was a man, "How could I forget?" They laughed, being silly and they knew it. "I like the way you look." Pause. "I saw your pin."

"Yes."

"And you need some sun. Here," and with a hop to his knees, dug fingers into a small coin pocket in his bikini, took the other's open hand with his free hand, as he, with his golden tan, cute nose, red lips, and dark brown eyes, dropped onto the palm, a clasped, gold-plated safety pin, over which he closed his hand, lifted the sun tan oil, and said,

"Let me do your back."

Triumph!

MISTER VALESQUEZ' handwriting was so firm and legible it was impossible to ignore, and once begun, a reward to read. He took such care. And as he read his poems, stories and essays aloud to the class, his teacher, a middle-aged white man named Robinson, often drifted over, and gazed down at the text, while, seated in his student desk chair, Mister Valesquez followed, word by word with his index finger, as he read aloud, even while Mister Robinson watched. Yet never for too long, before walking away, so as to show no preference. Robinson enjoyed handwritten manuscripts, and looked at every opportunity. Gained insights. In that prison classroom, one more clue in the mystery of teaching there. Mister Valesquez, for example, enjoyed writing by hand, and the act of erasing. Burns did too. The other guys hated it. *Hated* it! Lines and lines of words made up of letters, connected, and spelled right! Unfair! Frustrating! Until Robinson told them what a sentence was, and then paragraphs. Aw yeah. Hey. Unh huh.

Mister Valesquez had been amazed that the rewrite should be done on a separate, clean sheet of paper, having taken it for granted he write on a page made clean by erasing. Robinson agreed that was okay, but why work so hard erasing so much? Why not draw a line through and to hell with it? And with his permission, using Mister Valesquez' text, Robinson copied the section under discussion on the blackboard, including the debatable line, through which, after he finished, Robinson drew one long chalk line talking as he did so: "This means 'Take it out,' or 'delete.'" Writing the word "delete" on the blackboard, explaining the marginal notation, which Mister Valesquez and the other guys copied. "So," Robinson went on, "on your rewrite, use a clean sheet of paper, and copy from the first, corrected—"

"Draft," Valesquez grinned.

"Copy," Temple Burns said.

"Right," Robinson smiled, to Valesquez, turning to Burns, who didn't smile, which Robinson had learned meant nothing. Burns was a complex man, a black orphan on the defense, wanting to help his people. A bond had formed, for Burns had begun the semester by writing essays and editorials for the prison newsletter, urging black, nay all inmates to take advantage of in-prison educational opportunities, thus giving them a chance for intellectual discourse and dialogue which both men enjoyed.

Robinson had encouraged rewriting, using professional proofreader and copy editing signs and language while suggesting that of the two evils: overwriting and underwriting, overwriting was preferred, for it was easier to delete than insert. Deletion kept the rhythms alive, insertions tended to interrupt, risking a complete rewrite. Thus stressing the value of a top quality first draft, to lessen lengthy rewrites. Also, keep manuscripts easy to read. A clean rewrite saves an editor, agent and typesetter a lot of unnecessary work. The final draft presented should be as clean as possible no matter how many copies it takes. This stuff, while he talked, was written on the blackboard, and the guys copied.

So.

Mister Valesquez had come to class with a new poem, two pages long, handwritten, on lined paper. A dream, for fact, which he had written as a poem, in part rhyme, in part not.

It concerned a beautiful woman in a garden who at end faded away to reappear as "a flower," and as so often the case with poetry, the poet's voice held his audience captive, but, aside from it, Robinson knew a silent reading of the text would reveal what he called potholes that would demand a rewrite. Mister Valesquez had in classes past agreed: it, was done on the spot. But as Mister Robinson looked over his shoulder as Mister Valesquez read, Robinson made a mental note, and after the poem was over and the guys agreed they liked it, Robinson complimented Mister Valesquez on his reading it so well, but perhaps it was, unfinished? Some squabbling, Robinson insisting it was unfinished, he didn't say it was *bad,* it was incomplete, and needed a rewrite which Mister Valesquez might do for the next class? Fill in the potholes? Hm?

Amusement.

In steady defense of his poem, however, Mister Valesquez suggested, perhaps Mister Robinson didn't understand? Mister Robinson did indeed understand, and all that was said was understood, but potholes remained in the poem, on the paper, and after a continued quarrel almost creating a standoff because Mister Valesquez could not believe his poem was not as it was to him, it was so much so that *it was what it was,* what esle could it be? — paper raised in his left hand, his right index finger pointing at it, Valesquez bared his teeth, big grin: "*This* is what *it* IS!" which was true, and Robinson agreed, and Mister Valesquez was right, but the words did not say so, Mister Valesquez said so, which Mister Valesquez thought was funny, and he laughed, amused. BUT, in the end, after much wrangling, he agreed to rewrite it. And he did. Next class walked in, sat down with a smile, and after Smiley, the School Block C.O. took attendance, Mister Valesquez said he had done the rewrite. Good. Robinson asked him to read it, and Mister Valesquez read the same poem as it was before with conviction, to everyone's surprise.

"I thought you did a rewrite," Robinson said, baffled.

"I did!" cried Valesquez, insulted. "Here!" He held it up, and shook it. "Here it is!"

Robinson had his lips parted to ask why he hadn't read it? Read *that* copy? Valesquez saw his face.

"You mean I should read from the rewrite?"

Robinson nodded.

Valesquez gave Robinson a look of reproach, followed by one of disdain, above a growing smile, because he liked his teacher.

"You did not tell me that." Pause. "I thought I would show you, after I read the first draft."

Pause. Robinson embarrassed. "You're right. I — I should have told you. I'm sorry." Pause. "Would you read it?"

"Yes."

Valesquez read the rewrite. The guys could tell he was happy with it. It was good. Clear — no potholes. No bad ones, anyway, with its dream-quality intact, and at the end, which he had not written before, thus it was discovered in the rewrite, the beautiful woman in the garden who had faded away to reappear as "a flower," returned in the rewrite a rose. Robinson —

"What color!"

Valesquez: "Red!"

"Write it in!"

Done!

"How did it smell?"

"Sweet!"

Robinson's right hand swept toward Mister Valesquez, who, amid classroom laughter as well as his own, which shook his body, wrote the word in, and held up the sheet of paper, poem complete, his eyes bright, cheeks flushed, and read aloud —

> ". . . and in my hand appeared
> a sweet red rose."

So

SMALL, HEAVY-BREASTED woman with narrow shoulders and waist under a blunt, black face: big eyes, little nose, round mouth with thin, creased lips, and having been a Corrections Officer going on her third Christmas at the prison, her eyes were shifty, wasn't sure of herself anyway, against her shining black skin, dark eyes in white snapped left and right as if on strings, snap! Snap! Those sidelong glances, much like the convicts, in fact, over whom she had the power of her whim, and the laws of the land.

Prison guards — Corrections Officers — weren't sure of themselves either, nor of her, save that she was there, to exercise her duty, as well as the prison's rules, sure of herself with her government behind her, she might as well be white, like the rest of the black Officers, in doing her job felt she was not a black person but a person, and being a person being a prison guard who wasn't black was being white: being white was being power. The white guards knew, in a never ending game for control: black Officers had fast jive that embarrassed if not humiliated the white Officers, but the white Officers had the power, so white Officers imitated black jive and black Officers imitated white power, once in a while getting nasty, every so often it was fun, nasty fun after work, with guns, to bars and booze, and perhaps to bed, though bed not so often as bars, nor bars so often as nasty, which was more common than fun, itself rare enough, for even fun was hostile, in its way, as the fun after sex, or the fear, and uncertainty, so, never certain, as behind a veil, in an illusion of having a job and getting along together — action after work, as well as before, meaning on the way home from work, and being at home. Waking up. On the way to work. And being at work, with each other. After work every day, in a secret outline of living with guns and walls and bars for a nine to five he took off his .38 before he undressed, she did too, in the motel, each placing weapons on the bedside table beside glasses, pitcher of water, bucket of ice, fifth of Johnny Walker Black Label in a power switch to jive above an abyss of fantasy that held them suspended for high tension reasons as real as their lives: release, violence, sex and murder. Always murder.

Always.

"*Always,*" death whispered, with an echo, "*Always, always.*"

101

Always.

On the very sight of him she creamed, and lost control.

Bad man, bad kid from the beginning oh boy how handsome, how daring, how clever, smart, and tough, a neighborhood legend: her idol—every girl's idol, and if he had smiled to her, and had said hi, she melted, as she had melted, like the other girls, boys too, his smile and greeting was an honor, his every wish obeyed, his laughter rang down dark ghetto streets, in a low curse, twinkle of knife blade, silent step, gone into shadows. Sunny afternoons in a three-piece suit, picking pockets at the stock exchange, at parties to steal jewelry and rape women in back yards or back alleys. Daring, clever, smart, brutal, he nonetheless established a pattern of robbery and rape, and though feared by police safe in their squad cars, tough—smart—detectives set a trap and caught him.

Not one or two but three Officers saw her approach him as he stood in the prison line of new men, waiting to be given clothes, as guards saw the comic theatre of her being casual, just saying hello, as his presence was so magnetic she almost drooled, her eyes glazed,

"Hi," she said. "Remember me?"

He turned, looked down, blinked, said, "Hey, sure! How are—*baby*," teeth from ear to ear: "What are *you*, doing *here*?"

"Well," likewise, yet shifty-eyed: "How about *you*?"

Pleasant laughter. Nothing unusual, prison guards and convicts from the same neighborhood—their eyes met.

"See you around," she said.

"I'm not going anywhere," he replied, moving forward in the line, not watching her walk away, he knew, she knew, so did the other Officers: he had made a very good contact.

"Tonight," she whispered to him, a few days later, no one seeing her.

At the mercy of her whim what could he do but agree? in a whisper,

"*Okay.*"

In her compulsion she thought no one knew, but, between other guards, and between the convict snitches, and anybody with a brain in their head knew she was hot for that guy—hotter than hot—it had become a cell block game to see how long she could go, and how nasty she became! and yet funny, too, according to mood, around midnight talked her way in, telling Officers about her friend from the neighborhood, aw come on, and after a while they said okay, to tease

102

her, string her along, playing the game, she was inside, and walking soft, down along the row of dark cells, to his, whispered his name, unlocked the cell door, slipped in as he woke realizing who it was, glad with a happy heart she was there, they went right to it, getting what she had wanted from all the way back on the street, hoping, in those days to be lucky enough to catch his eye, in sudden glare of flashlights, black and white voices, barking, as the Warden stepped forward the laws of the land behind him, to interrupt with secret glee, and righteous indignation, to her:

"Get your things together, clear out your locker and get out. You're through."

The Warden turned, so too his lieutenants. They marched away, footsteps echoing, keys jangling.

The Officers who had witnessed the interruption were as impressed and amused as the rest of the cell block, which was in pandemonium. Officers impressed because they couldn't do what that convict did in that cell. But amused that he did, and got that far. So, in awe of him, there in his cell where she had gone to give herself, and of course because neither they nor the Warden would do such a thing it was funny in such an outrageous, point blank, fact — bang! doing it with him, *there* seeming *so* bizarre, so, the Officers were nice to her, stayed with her and joked, wishing her well from her wall locker to the front door, in their strange, convoluted racist's respect, and their envy, which was why they had informed the Warden right away, and he had waited on call, after the snitches had also informed him.

*   *   *

Toward the end of the following June, with the big 4th of July weekend coming up, the small suburban bank, set back from the main street of town, under trees, was doing good business, and as middle-class Americans lined up before tellers to make deposits or take out money for the holidays, a small black woman in dark blue uniform moved among them, directing customers to proper windows for savings, or the fastest line for cashing checks, by way of helping out, maybe putting people off, for in her shining black face dark eyes in white snapped left and right as if on springs, snap! Snap! Those sudden sidelong glances, lightning fast, on every person on the marble-patterned floor, she stood with a fixed smile, near a tall, potted plant, beside the low railing which separated the public from the polished desks of busy men and women officers of the bank.

Night

IN A CITY anywhere, USA.

A middle-aged couple walking along a sidewalk by a park, a city park. The night was warm, and in the darkness beneath branches of maple trees, the scent of fresh cut grass. A breeze touched their cheeks.

The center of the park was a circular area, couples sat on the edge of a sparkling water fountain. Someone played an electric guitar. Cars rolled by on asphalt streets. Winos slept on benches. People walked dogs. Lovers kissed in shadows. The middle-aged couple spoke in a low, intimate tone. She in denim jacket, white shirt, jeans and sneakers. He too, yet without jacket. A folded newspaper in his left hand, she with shoulder bag. Across the park from them, a squad car was parked by the opposite entrance. Its presence reassuring. Driver's window open. Thick elbow on sill. In cigarette glow, part of his face appeared, went dark. A younger couple passed, each pushing a pram. Boys and girls laughed in a passing taxi, a dog barked, out of the shadows a running young man was before them, seized her bag, spun her around as she raised her arm, and fell, striking her hip and shoulder on the sidewalk as the other, in a flash, met the eyes of her husband—dashed away, her bag in hand.

The man dropped to his knees to help his wife, thinking to call to the thief, *There's nothing in the bag! Drop it!* but the sight of his wife trying to get to her feet—all in a wink—he helped her up.

"I'm all right," she said. Rubbed her shoulder. "Nothing serious."

But someone had seen, and called out. The squad car raced off in the same direction the thief had gone, to turn left on the avenue, and cut him off.

"Go," she said, "forget about the bag. Follow him. I know you want to." She sat on a bench. "I'm okay," with a smile. *"Go! Come back and tell me!"*

He dashed to the water fountain, dipped his handkerchief in, returned to her—

"Thanks, dear. Be quick!"

On the corner of the avenue, to which he ran as fast as he could, in pretty good shape! he got there, heard the blood-chilling shriek of brakes, a thump, and saw, as he stood, panting, the body of the thief, but a boy, turning over and over in midair into oncoming traffic, in descent her bag in his hand, struck the front of an airport limo, bounced to its left to strike the side of a speeding taxi, and fall, crumpled, bouncing to a halt as brakes screamed, tires squealed, alert drivers avoiding a pair of three car collisions, all this being at an intersection, as the light changed, and traffic crossed, avoiding the body of the boy in the middle of the avenue. The man ran toward him, knelt there. The boy looked up, a black boy, in faded green t-shirt, designer jeans, Nike sneakers, shoe strings untied, t-shirt soaked with sweat, face and arms glistened. The right side of his face bloody meat, other cheek down, on asphalt. Right arm bent the other way, breathing hard. Body lumpy. Lips parted, eyes wide, terrified, legs twitching, jerking, trapped, trying to break out, in a last, wild, run to freedom.

Siren and squad car approached, the man looked around, saw the car slow, and in the glare of headlights, stop. Two uniformed officers got out, began walking toward the boy, one reaching for a pair of handcuffs, in the rising siren whoop of an approaching ambulance, the boy's body jerked in terror, eyes bugged out for he recognized the man, fingers let go of the strap of the bag, the man moved in such a way his body blocked the officers' view, as he picked it up, rose to his feet with it tucked under his arm. The officers joined him.

"You won't need handcuffs," he said.

"Just in case," stepping forward, leaned over the boy, stretched out his hands to bring both the boy's hands behind his back—

"No! Look at his arm!"

The officer did, and seeing it, nodded, rising, gazed down and shook his head.

The ambulance snuck into the crowd, for a crowd had gathered, the way ambulances sneak in, howling the announcement of their effort, siren sinking to a low *beeeeeooop,* and silence. Two paramedics got out, and walked toward the boy.

"You'll need a stretcher," the man said.

Made them speechless, in fury, didn't *they* know? The man knew this, and was amused, because he was angry. An officer asked him—

"Hey. Are you the guy this kid robbed?"

"My wife. But yes."

"Want to come to the station to press charges?"

"No."

"Why not?"

"He gave it back to me," holding out the bag, yet indicating the

106

two characters coming toward them with a stretcher, looked square into the eyes of the officer, and said,

"Tell them to be gentle with the boy."

The officer parted his lips to speak, but could find no words, and watched the man turn, walk toward, into and through the crowd, away into the night.

The officer crossed to the paramedics, helped them wheel the stretcher close to the boy's body, and—the other officer, startled, also helped. The four lifted him, the first officer saying *Easy, easy does it. Watch it!* They lowered him on, yet he rather tumbled, and as they rolled the stretcher toward the open rear doors of the ambulance, and he was lifted inside with the officers helping at every step, the boy closed his eyes, and began to whimper.

Soon the doors were closed, a medic sat across from the boy, the engine started, siren howling, whooping the ambulance moved through the dispersing crowd, gathered speed, mad racket rising, to the nearest public hospital. The two police officers sat in their squad car, filled out forms and radioed in the report which would be filed and coordinated with information received from the official hospital inquiry. The squad car returned to its station, at the entrance to the park. The two officers sat in the front seat, talking, and smoking cigarettes, although one of them, he behind the wheel, thick elbow on the open sill, was yet a little shaken, in an inner way he could not put into words, and found himself in an unknowing way, searching the park, with his policeman's eyes, part of his face seen in cigarette glow, as a scent of petunias on a breeze crossed his cheek reminded him of soft lights, a woman's voice, a warm and downy pale blue fabric, and rough, large, secure hands, eyes searching, maybe he'd see him again.

It

THE SUBURBAN FALL SEASON appeared in its usual beauty unnot-
iced save by eccentrics, for as leaves tumbled down in late September,
the blue exhaust fumes from cars driven by highschool boys racing
to play football matched the shade of blue of cigarette smoke in liv-
ingrooms nationwide, all eyes watching television, for America either
played football, or watched with zeal, hearts pounding, teeth bared,
bug-eyed: *kill 'em!* as a quarterback sank back, his line held steady,
ends raced out, *break 'em up!* cocked his arm to throw, *crush 'em!* a gunship rose over a jungle village, *murder 'em!* .50 caliber shells lashed
down, he threw a bullet, hit his target, shattering the faces of women
and children, brains and mud for a ten yard gain the crowd went wild
at home or on the field.

And some wanted in.

A strong and handsome high-school junior weighing 130 pounds,
with long curly brown hair, a clean smile, and piercing glassy blue
Paul Newman eyes: also wanted in, and she was a girl, but she wanted
to play, on the team.

In a nation where cooperation was crushed by competition, why
not? Weren't the people free to make up their minds and do what
their rich leaders wished, and the media told them? Of course. She
could join the Army, why not play football? Thus that afternoon, after
school, as she in uniform walked toward the field — field deserted, she
was early for practice, coaches and team in the locker room getting
dressed. She approached the bleachers. Three of her teammates appeared, in uniform, big guys, each held a football. Their faces were
funny.

"Hi," she smiled, "I — I must be early."

"Yeah."

"Must be."

The third was silent, as the first threw the ball into her face, the
second ball hit her throat, and as the third hit her cheek the first boy
hit her in the mouth with his fist as the second struck her stomach,
the third kicked her shins. She fell. They gathered round, kicked her,
spat on her, reached down and slapped her, dragged her onto the field,
and threw blocking dummies at her before melting out of sight as the
team appeared, she was curled up, panting, choking tears, humiliated,
outraged, determined not to tell, yet later did as her parents would

not have silence. Thus the story got out, and hit the wire services, the local network picked it up and there she was on the 6 o'clock news, embarrassed out of mind, only able to murmur. Cut to camera on field, the coach told how he and the team had found her, he pointed down to his feet, said, "Here is where she was."—Cut to principal who scowled, spoke of democracy, freedom of individual rights, and punished the boys with a flourish: each boy benched for the game coming up, a big game, an important game.

The first boy's father joked with the principal.

"You know how boys are, ha ha, roughed her up a little, just kidding around."

"Yes," the principal replied, adjusting his rimless glasses, "I understand. I know. But you don't know what happened. Reporters broke into my office. I was at work at my desk. School was closed. How did they get in? They wanted a statement. 'A statement?' I asked. 'About what?' They told me. I didn't know what they were talking about. They forced me into the corridor, bright lights, cameras, reporters with microphones, if coach MacMahon hadn't shown up, I—I might have gone mad, or fainted, or both."

*   *   *

The boy's father knew his son had lied to him, yet there was little father could do, hadn't he brought the boy up to be a liar, a cheat and to do what *he* had never dared but *oh boy wanted to*: beat up a dumb broad who wanted to play football, spit on her, be glad she got *spit!* hadn't he spoken of women with disgust and impatience? letting the boy in on those dumb four letter words as the gunship banked, and came around, thinking *they* know what *they* want, the gunner fixing sights on the native girl, think they can *take what we got* and do *anything they want* running down the dirt road to the river, the automatic machine gun swiveled, tracked its victim and in a mad clatter went into action, as the gunner watched bullets kick up dust spots on the way to the girl's heels, and rip up her spine, fling her corpse head over heels into a heap, on the road, as the gunship swept upward, and the gunner looked out over the jungle. The pilot laughed. The gunner smiled. The weapon, dog-like, lowered its snout. Its master sat back, not much of a gain, that girl, in a game like this. The sky was blue. And the field beyond the cloudless space was deserted, in a distant echo of the roar of the crowd, fading, as an anthem into silence, hidden behind the blank screen of a television set turned off, alone, like God, in the corner of a living room, deep in the darkness of a sleeping house on the edge of a cliff, above a vast and restless sea.

110

SUPREME COURT DEFENDS
50% RACIAL EQUIVALENCE IN
NATIONWIDE POLICE DEPARTMENTS

DADE COUNTY, FLORIDA. A squadcar parked at an intersection. Two figures in the front seat. A young, black rookie behind the wheel. An experienced white officer beside him.

"Look!" cried the rookie. "They-at Ga-reen Taur-us we-ent by at 75!"

"Yay-uh," smiled the other. "Wanna chay-ace it? G'wan! I'll watch!"

"The spee-ed limmit is fifty-fahv!"

"Evvybuddy drahves fas' done heah, doan worra-abouddit."

"Is th' *law*!"

"Evvybuddy breaks th' *law, evvy*buddy, evin me. So wha'."

"Look! A cah wi' ta-one headlaht!"

"Tay me anotha'."

"B-b-but somewnna passin' maht thank izza motacahcle, n' git kill'!"

"Wal, go *git* 'im. Giv' 'im a tickit!"

"O-key, ah git it."

"Les git th' bastahds we kin ketch, ya wanna chase popahyes all naht?"

"How else am Ah gonna becum-a dick-tecktiv'?"

Pause. "Check those thray vay-ans ovah they-ah," his voice low. "By-ah Wahl-green's."

111

Um.

"Lit's go."

The rookie phoned in coded location, number and target. The squad car pulled into traffic.

Three black Chevy vans, outside Walgreen's.

The driver of the first van got out, and entered the store.

The driver of the second got out, walked around, bent over, and inspected the front bumper.

The driver of the third van got out, walked around and opened the rear doors. Waited on the sidewalk. She was a blonde, with a nice tan, in a lime green dress, dark blue canvas sandals, and white-rimmed dark glasses. She lit a cigarette. In the glow of the butane flame, for night was upon them, her dark glasses reflected twin images of the squad car, entering the parking lot, across the mall in shadows where it turned left, and crept along a row of palm trees toward her.

Funny

HE HAD ten dollars. Ten.

There was a sale on coffee beans. $3.99 a pound. Buy two, get one free—the store brand, of course. But if that's what she wanted, that's what he'd get her.

So, realizing he had no umbrella, he rose from his desk, put on his coat and hat, and with a wink to switchboard, went out in the rain, heading up the avenue towards the store. Wasn't raining very hard, more mist with a little drizzle. Hat down, collar up, step step step. Liked to walk fast. Middle-aged guy, nice looking. On his lunch break.

Step step step.

Passed several street vendors, their display tables all in a row, the last selling umbrellas, the large, colorful kind he hadn't been able to find. So asked the husky Oriental gentleman behind the display—of scarves, gloves, hats of all kinds. Umbrellas. Eight dollars.

The fellow's blue van parked by the curb, and he, therefore, between van and display. Another Oriental gentleman got out of the van, and joined him.

"No. Sorry," the customer said.

"No?"

"No. Can't afford it."

"*You?*" Surprised. Both laughed. Skeptics.

"You rich fella."

"Got *lots* money."

He grinned as they smiled, their eyes teasing.

Bingo!

Had an idea.

This was street theater. A part of big city life, like pollution, poverty, crime, hookers, noise, sirens, police and fire engines, so too street peddlers.

"Listen," he said, leaning forward, looking both guys in the eyes, first one then the other, he made a small smile,

"I don't have enough money."

"Eight dollar? You? Ha ha!"

He held up a hand. Laughed with them. "I know," he agreed. "I know, but I don't have enough. I look like I do." Low smile,

115

looking at them. "I look like I've got it, but," shaking his head, shoulders raised, "I don't."

Stepped back, looking at them. Right at them. No smile. Well, a little one, be agreeable.

They looked back at him. Right back. The skepticism faded, their teasing eyes changed, their faces went deadpan as they got it, and he waved, turned away, and walked up the avenue, step step step, with much inner laughter.

At the corner he turned. Looked back. Both were laughing, out loud. Ha ha ha! Oh it didn't happen often, one should never count on it! But every so often, ah yes, a white man understood.

The Dream

DR. HENRY, noted psychiatrist, and his friend Dexter (lovers for as long as I can remember), were out for supper with their friend Sheila, and her young lover, Andy.

It was a small, quiet, velvet curtained, candlelit Greek place near the flower district.

Midway through the meal, a man, drinking at the bar, turned, and seeing Dr. Henry, rose from his barstool, crossed between tables toward them, and stood, a pleasant-faced businessman, in tweed jacket, white shirt, looking down.

"Excuse me," the stranger said, "You're Dr. Henry. I know I'm interrupting your meal—"

"You are," Dexter growled, middle-aged. Shaggy. "Yes. You are!"

"—but," ignoring, "may I—I a-a-ask one question?"

Dr. Hen—his nickname—smiled.

In a grimace of pain, the other stammered—

"Why do I-I laugh like o-o-other men? Men whom I-I don't like a-at *all*?" Pause. "Almost a-all my life?"

"Almost?"

"All right, *a-all* my life!"

The fellow's face flushed, and contorted in the effort to speak. Everyone interested.

People at nearby tables turned. Hen:

"Because you're impressionable. The reason why might not be hard to discover. Here's my card. Call if you wish, and make an appointment." Small white lips smiled, under direct, round eyes. "We'll dig into it."

"Ah—thank you!"

The gentleman, yet blushing, tucking card into shirt pocket, returned to the bar, finished his drink, and departed in that way as if on having entered he had forgotten to leave, and seeing Dr. Hen reminded him.

"What was that about?" Sheila asked, being AA, sipped Perrier.

"Insecurity," Hen said.

"Yes, that's clear, but—"

"Who is secure these days? The man has a stammer, he imitates other men? And," poignant look, "he's creative."

117

"Meaning?"

"Life today very difficult for the insecure creative, wouldn't you agree? Isn't insecure creativity the first victim of a fascist takeover?"

"They don't know what creativity is."

"Insecure creativity," murmured Dexter, "is an economic failure, therefore useless. Therefore, first cutbacks. But the secret reason for it, is insecure or not insecure, creative people are latent idealists, and exercise a conscious morality, and we all know—" gazing round the table—"what the right wing would do with creative, moral idealists."

"First, cut off their money."

"Stalin knew what to do."

Andy was about to explode.

"But why," shooting a glance at Sheila for approval, "why laugh like someone he *hated*?"

Hen forked *dolmathes avgolemono,* as his dark eyes, large, and wide, held contact with the other's.

"Maybe he was jealous."

Andy lowered his eyes, his face burning, yet raised them in challenge—

"Why *laugh* like them?"

"Maybe that's what they had in common."

"They?"

"The men he's been jealous of."

Anger. "I don't understand."

"You were never jealous of someone funnier than you? A friend—or enemy? Someone, for example"—leaning forward, his high thin face, and wide round eyes shining in candlelight—"someone who could tell jokes better than you, who could charm all the boys and girls, and make them laugh with his wit, hm?"

Knife and fork in hand poised midair, youthful eyes gazed beyond, in gathering realization, tips of two front teeth between red lips—

"I see," he whispered, and lowered his eyes.

The table noticed in a quiet warmth, for in growing awareness and comprehension, emotions flickered across the young man's face, visible to all. Sheila's eyes misted. Andy—

"What's everybody so *quiet* about!"

Adult amusement. Sheila wiped her eyes. Dexter lowered his hand, stroked Hen's thigh. They rubbed knees.

Over coffee, Sheila asked,

"Well, Doctor, any ideas on this Mid-Eastern mess?"

Hen looked at Dexter, who spoke in a low, husky voice,

118

"In an essay in the middle 1950s, Bertrand Russell predicted that location for World War III, the reason being oil. Add the horror of Palestinian displacement, plus a power-crazed, totalitarian Israel, and—" glanced at Hen.

"We go to work for peace. All of us."

Glasses raised all round. Against deep blue draperies with gold trim, Hen's tall head seemed to float, and the dome of his narrow, pink forehead glistened. Small white lips parted, and his large, round, yellow-banded coal black eyes blazed, in an expression of wonder, in the vision of the ideal:

"To peace!"

Dark Blue

A WHITE MAN with a paunch and messy gray hair, who was a little drunk that night, had gone out for another bottle, on orders from his girlfriend to hurry back: supper almost ready.

Great!

He walked a few smoggy blocks to a discount store run by a family from New Jersey. A franchise operation, one in a chain, where two not so young daughters, in skirts or slacks and long-sleeved white or light blue angora sweaters and thin gold bracelets, with their sly, seductive glances lined with mascara, were certain this man, this tipsy customer was crazy, remarking how pretty their sweaters were, they knew what he meant, and that's what they would think, from New Jersey with very little thought, while chewing gum, and selling pints of fortified wine to bums, and cheap blackberry brandy to little old ladies worth millions, counting pennies from worn, cloth purses, while toy poodles panted at their feet: *let's go! Let's go! Let's go!*

And to look around for a decent wine to have with supper, was a chore, for second rate, popular brands were displayed, and stocked above and below eye-level. Bottles had not been dusted, nor had shelves. Opened and closed cartons, and wood boxes were stacked at right angles to other displays, or in front of shelf stock, and made walking and looking difficult, while the two daughters and their brothers hung around the cash register at the front counter, behind a dusty front window, talking in the new minimal mode, using almost no words: funny little transparencies, cleaning and filing and painting fingernails, while chewing gum. Another sitcom, another slice of life. The ceiling seemed a little lower, walls a tint darker, the light became muted, as on an interior set, growing darker.

But in the soft pop of a small bubble they were gone, who took their place? A tall, middleaged Korean gentleman who spoke good English, and his daughter who, with baby smooth skin, composed features, and cautious dark eyes, spoke not at all.

The customer made his purchase, thanked her and departed, feeling, in an odd way, as though something had been going on behind his back, as he had stood at the counter, facing the Oriental girl.

A few days later in the same condition the man went in for the same reason, made his purchase from the silent girl, noticing she had broad shoulders and a very healthy, almost husky body in another realization that the light was brighter, the window behind her clean, all objects in the store, as he turned to look, sprang into view, each shining, every bottle in its place at eye-level on clean shelves, aisles cleared, ceiling a sparkling white.

The recognition crossing his face could not be missed, yet she was silent.

"Looking *good*!" he exclaimed.

She murmured something.

"How's business?" he joked.

She looked right at him, like a cat, face blank, as the corners of her mouth went up, like the tails of inverted commas, to the tune of that same little murmur.

"Swell," he said. But the famous, or stereotyped Oriental humor, was absent from her eyes, as this teasing Yankee smiled, she looked at him as at a passport photo: *I have never seen this man before except once.*

Her gaze was so cold and remote, and her face so still she looked as unreal as a camera. Glad he had had those drinks! Doing business with this cookie was a tough job! Therefore, thanking her, he took a step toward the door, noticing a radio and realizing he had in fact heard a voice say Beethoven, and not believing his ears, looked, and there was a radio on the top shelf under the window, and a voice was talking about the next selection, by Beethoven.

"Do you like music?"

She squeaked. (Yes.)

Man: "Mozart and Beethoven?"

Girl: Nod.

Man: "Which?"

She didn't answer. Eyes cold.

"Do you have a favorite?" he asked, preferring Mozart and about to say so but changed his mind, and asked, "What do you like best of Beethoven?" Fast pause. "The quartets?"

She shook her head. Her lips parted and a girl's voice came out and said,

"The piano concertos."

sending his eyebrows up and jiggling his jaw, he said,

"Oh!"

before he said the first syllable beginning with M, and adding an o, she said,

"The symphonies," and he said zart, which he thought was funny and she did not and he laughed. Her smile crept out in her cheeks

122

a little, and her eyes although warming somewhat, stayed remote.

"Did you know," he asked, "that Neville Marriner with Alfred Brendel has recorded all the Mozart piano concertos?"

She raised her eyes and stared into space.

Her father drifted into view, bright-eyed and smiling, to join her behind the counter.

She looked at the customer. "I know Brendel," she said, meaning his recordings.

"Did you know that Neville Marriner has conducted and recorded, in one package, *all* the Mozart symphonies?"

She looked at him.

"That is interesting."

"Yes," the customer smiled. "On Phillips CD. I have them at home, on tapes."

"Yes. On Phillips. I think I have heard that."

"Did you know Mozart was eight years old when he wrote his first symphony?"

"Yes."

"You *did?*"

"She's a student at Juilliard," her father said.

Glancing from father to daughter, with a funny smile the customer leaned forward, and as the daughter looked at him with cool, and amused tolerance, he said,

"So here you are," with a grin, "a student at Juilliard, selling booze to these crazy creeps and bums on Second Avenue, right?"

"RIGHT!" she yelled.

Laughed. Father too, so too the customer, who patted the pint in his jacket pocket, and with a wave, thanked them, and laughing, walked outside leaving them so amused, standing behind the shining plate glass window of their clean, bright store, as he walked away, deep into the labyrinth, of the tall, dark blue city.

YES!

CHEWING GUM and smoking a cigarette, Darlene went into the living room to ask her father to lower the volume of the television set, because she was doing her homework. Her father, seen in profile, right eye protruding from his head, as — for the lights were low — the colors from the screen danced across his face, had a reptilian cast: mouth open, lower lip hung. Raised a Bud to the oral hole, but paused, leaned forward, left hand in a fist, murmuring pleas, and snarling one- two-syllable words. Quarterback fumbled. Lost the ball. Other team recovered: first and ten on their own forty-seven. Her father put the can — a pint — of Bud on the coffeetable before him, in between a glass bowl of potato chips beside a wooden dish of nuts by a small cutting board with a half crumbled block of cheddar cheese, knife, and a box of salted crackers.

"What happened?" she asked, standing at the side of his deep, upholstered chair.

He told her.

It looked bad. With so few minutes left, their team ahead by six fragile points, and, although the game had been well-played, it was certain the other team would score, and with a field goal, take the game. The big one. The one America waited for. The Super Bowl.

"Daddy, could ya lower th' soun'? I gotta study fuh a test."

"Yuv had all weeken'!" Pushed a button on the remote control, sound lowered. But he was angry. Because she indeed had had all weekend, and he knew that after she finished her schoolwork she would go out again, as she had on Friday night, and last night, with her friends, and hang out somewhere, doing what she would do, God knew what, but so far hadn't come home pregnant. And in an odd way, like this, in this mulish way, they were alike. Super Bowl or not, she said she had to study, and it was true, so she did study. Like her father she was thick-waisted, with plump rosy cheeks, sensual lips, and dark curly hair. Acne on her cheekbones. Dark eyes veiled.

She closed the door to her room, and as she sat down at her desk, heard a yell. Her father. Again. Her mother's outcry —

Darlene opened her door, took a few steps down the narrow corridor, and dashed into the living room. Saw her mother reeling backwards, her hands before her face as the edge of the glass bowl of potato chips, chips flying, split her upper lip, cracked and chipped her front teeth, and bounced on an angle to shatter against a wall as the pint of Bud hit the bridge of her nose like a fastball — and spun away. Beer ran down her face, mixed with blood, and streamed off her chin, onto her blouse, skirt and the rug, as Darlene's father screamed, *screamed* that they had lost as in background fans shrieked, sound of remote cheers, her father, his hands out before him, face purple with rage, he'd lost five hundred dollars, couldn't she understand?

Turned off the tv, crossed to the hall door, opened a closet, put on a hunting jacket, scarf and cap and left.

Darlene got her mom together best as possible, but the split lip would not stop bleeding. She called a taxi. Took her mom to the emergency room at All County, both women anxious that their family doctor not be on duty, as he worked there one night a week.

Inside the cab.

"Yuh okay, Ma?"

"Yeh, honey. Yuh'm angel."

Darlene recalled last year, Super Bowl. She had gone out with her friends, came home late. Next day saw Ma had a black eye . . . Ma and dad hadn't said anything.

"He lost *five hunner' dollahs*?"

"I don' tink suh," Ma said, holding a tissue against her lip. "He meant he stood tuh win it, yuh know. Th' ferth quarta, th' score bein' wha' i' t'was."

"Yeh," Darlene said, remembering the gambling pool the guards had, in the prison. "Why'd he blame yuh?"

"Had tuh blame somebody." Pause. "I hope er doctuh ain't on duty." Pause. "Doctuh Perry."

"Me too." Pause. "Yeh." Pause. "Yeh."

Doctor Perry.

Darlene wanted to take Ma to the clinic, get her lip fixed up, and go home. Period. Yet she realized that as anxious and embarrassed as she was about going to the hospital — she knew Ma felt the same — underneath, she was afraid of her father. But she would fight for her mother, and — be humiliated by it all. The taxi pulled to a stop alongside a sidewalk, for the parking lot was full. Hospital very busy. An ambulance passed them, siren diminishing, and backed into its designated zone.

*   *   *

The corridor outside the Emergency Room was crowded, as in war, and Doctor Perry, a tall, thin young fellow in white coat, was tending to injured ladies of all ages and races, his long, thin, artistic fingers touching flesh, here and there, as he frowned, muttering to himself.

"Hi, Dar," he frowned. "Find a seat, be with you soon as I can," raising a purple eyelid of an older woman, curled up on a mobile stretcher, whimpering. Her left arm, broken at the elbow. Doc shone the beam of a small flashlight into the eye, bit his lip and scowled, switched off the light and stood erect. Noted on her chart that the white of her eye was bruised, and the outer edge of the iris crushed. Doc went to the next patient, a young black girl, on crutches.

Darlene and her mom found seats, curved plastic shells on an iron frame. Sounds came from inside, and in the corridor, the women, with members of their family — no men — beside them, some smoking cigarettes. The sobbing, bitter weeping, moans, curses and expressions of rage, suggested a world of battered women.

The resident psychiatrist passed through. Doc stopped him, asked —

"What are you doing here?"

"We had a meeting."

"What do you think?" With a gesture to the corridor.

"I think it's football. It happens every season, and this year's the same, but," with raised eyebrows, and narrowed eyes, "it's getting worse." Pause. "Americans love violence: the Super Bowl becomes an expression of home life. Bowl is just an 'e' away from the heart of the matter. I've got to go. Have a nice night, doctor."

That dialogue happened quite near Darlene, she heard every word, and whispered, "Yeh." Pause. "Yeh." Pause. "Yeh." Stared. Her father's face appeared before her, in profile, as if watching tv, bug-eyed, colors on the screen crossing his face. Can of Bud poised, before dangling lower lip, glint of wet lower teeth. "Daddy," Darlene asked: "Whadda me and Ma gonna do?" She closed her eyes. Her father turned, and looked at her. Right at her. She opened her eyes. Perspiration appeared on her forehead, and as her mother squeezed her hand, Darlene squeezed back, beholding the scene in the corridor. And one by one, every hair on her head stood on end, in a smell of his beery breath, within a huge, rising, accumulating roar of voices, in dismay.

She slumped down in her chair.

Her father's face disappeared.

"Jeepers," she murmured, her dark eyes sad: "What an asshole."

127

Bebe

SHE WAS AN ATTRACTIVE young woman, who had had a bad scene with drugs, tried to kill herself, and as part of her rehabilitation, was seeing Dr. Henry once a week. Her mother, with whom she lived, had money. She didn't like her mother. Her father had left them — for another woman. Dr. Henry's patient hadn't loved her father, oh liked him well enough, and missed him, and was hurt, and depressed that he hadn't missed her at all, nor her sister. Father was a dark, closed space which she resented and, in secret envied. It had come up in therapy that she envied him, being able to leave, as she would like to do, with, like him, no looking back. But that he didn't care had hurt, and had been much of the cause for her drug habit.

Dr. Henry had reminded her that as long as she was dependent on her mother — paying even for her therapy, she wouldn't be able to enjoy life on her own. Her mother liked having her at home and was more than willing to pay for, more or less anything, in the attempt to buy her way into her daughter's heart. That didn't work, for mother was material-minded and guilty, with little imagination. Sister was in Europe with a man, having a lot of fun, so it seemed.

Anyway, when Bebe told Dr. Hen about dreaming the word *Buxtehude,* and she didn't know what it meant, they talked about it and came up with *Bucks to hold,* and in the next session, after Bebe said she was looking for a job, Hen smiled —

"For some bucks to hold?"

Bebe didn't remember at first, but — "Do you think that's it?"

"Yes." Pause. "A little way your unconscious has, in telling you what it wants, too."

"You mean my unconscious wants to hold money?"

"Well, in its way, yes. Wants you to."

"But why?" Bebe amazed.

"Maybe there are things it wants, perhaps your getting an apartment of your own."

"Ha ha ha," Bebe laughed. "That's crazy!"

"Is it?" Hen smiled. Left eyebrow cocked.

She distrusted that. Narrowed her eyes. "Come on," she said. "What's on your mind?"

"Maybe your unconscious wants some space, to be free, it wants you to make a move—" he spread his hands. Yet the interpretation overwhelmed her, and as he understood, she blocked, and switched to a different track:

"I had another dream."

He nodded.

She knew what that meant: he was following.

"I dreamed my mother was having breakfast with Neville Marriner. You were there, too. I came downstairs and there you were, looking at them, at the table in the kitchen, having breakfast." She grinned. "Ha ha ha! How's that?" Winked. "Proof of my craziness?"

"Do you want me to answer that? Or do you want to?"

After some skull-cracking bear-like shrink tactics, Bebe got it.

"Yes," she said, near tears. "I would do that, just like me, isn't it. How in-character! Never dream that *I* would have breakfast with him, to begin *my* day, no, I give him to my mom."

"Yes. And if you had some bucks to hold maybe you'd get away from her, and dream of having breakfast with him, yes—" Dr. Hen leaned forward, eyes glowing, hands out, "a dream of music with a great conductor, who conducts, you see? You gave him to your mother because she is conducting your life: she's holding the bucks!"

Bebe wiped her eyes.

"You're right." Pause. "I'm gonna get a job!"

"Good."

As she left, and he greeted his next patient, Bebe yet turned, and looked back at him, for in a way she was in love with him and one day would learn that that was part of the rehabilitation, too, yet he glanced up, in a smile of farewell, and the warmth, kindness and understanding in his eyes ran deep in her, deep clear through, and she turned away, in a sudden sense of happiness, and fulfilment she hadn't experienced in memory. She made a deep resolution: her life would be affected, and her doctor would help her.

Being able to separate his patients as they came and went was of course part of his profession, yet the look on Bebe's face, and in her light blue eyes, was one of a new pride, and he was aware how beautiful her inner identity was, and as it moved outward and became her, he realized he would love her, but wasn't that part of his profession? The part so difficult to discuss, with anyone? Therefore, divided, he closed the door to his office, crossed the room with his new patient, and with professional skill, wiped his mind clear of the woman Bebe would become.

The Man

"DOCTUH PERRY? Sorry to botha yuh—"

"Is this Darlene?"

"Yeh. Whadda I do with my dad?"

"What's the matter?"

"He's kinda crazy."

"Because he hurt your mother?"

"Yeh. I think suh."

"What does he do?"

There was such an extended silence, the doctor asked,

"Are you there?"

"Yeh."

He realized she couldn't tell him.

"Can you talk to him?"

"*Talk* to 'im?"

"Yes. Talk to him. Try it. Let me know what he says. Would you like to see a psychiatrist?"

He heard her breath catch. "*Me? Why?*"

"Well, your father . . ."

"Whadda 'bout 'im?" Pause. "Huh?"

"Talk to him. Let me know what he says. Sorry, I have patients, thanks for calling. Feel free to call again. Good to hear your voice. Bye."

*   *   *

"Ma, I talked to Doctuh Perry."

"Yuh *did*! What for?"

"I tol' 'im about daddy."

"Yuh DID? Whud ya say?"

Darlene blushed, and told her. And what Doctor Perry had told her—to talk to him. She didn't mention the other.

"Talk tuh ya daddy?" Lips parted. "Whaddaya gonna say?"

Darlene shrugged.

But nobody talked to daddy, except to ask if he wanted something to eat, or, ya wanna nuddah Bud? Yeh gimme anudda.

What she wanted to say, or, rather, what she wanted to *know*, was why was he acting so crazy. If she asked him, however, he wouldn't be able to answer. Why, therefore, talk with him? But she didn't like it. Her friends couldn't help her—they understood, but they didn't know what to do either, for all their parents and homelife were similar, therefore, if they could ask the question they wanted, the answers could not be answered—in words, for aside from shared animal appetites and television, they didn't talk to each other.

*   *   *

"You're an unusual M.D."

"I had an interest in psychology—clinical psychology, in high school, and to be honest," Doctor Perry smiled, "I almost chose it for my profession."

"Why didn't you?"

"M.D.s are in my family. My aunt and sister are doctors." Pause. "My granddad was."

Roy Jones got a sleepy look, and his voice was low. "Unless we have rewarding private practices much of the romance and challenge is gone from the science." He paused. "In this hospital circumstance, my patients have limited health coverage, and certain diseases like alcoholism and drug abuse are out—too many people have those problems and it cost too much to cure them. The one safe area is hysteria."

"Why?"

"I can prescribe pills. Get it?"

"No."

"Drug companies like that."

"Are you a psychiatrist?"

"Yes." Pause. "I take it you like—Darlene?"

"I do," Perry frowned, "and I like her mom, too. Intelligent, sensitive people who don't know how to talk, thus play dumb. Dar chews gum, uses sloppy slang and keeps her face in a mask. If she could talk, there's a story there."

"You said she phoned you."

"Said her dad's acting crazy. What does that mean?" Roy Jones watched Perry's eyes try to see.

"What do you think?"

"He's violent. I'm convinced she and her mother are afraid."

"Tell her to call me."

"I told her to talk with her dad."

"What did she say?"

Perry laughed, as if self-conscious . . . "Well," in amusement, which was not amusement, and he was self-conscious, "I think she's

132

afraid to talk to him because she doesn't know how, yet if she did, he wouldn't know how to answer."

"What does he do?"

"A prison guard, out on the Island. Works in C-74."

"That's with adolescents." Pause. "Those guards are animals. A parole officer told me."

"Okay, he also drinks beer, a lot of beer, Budweiser, and watches television, nonstop until he passes out. I saw him once. He's unconscious and insecure."

"They're a type. Material-minded, too, therefore arrogant, and loud. Enjoy being bossed so they can be boss."

"Loves football."

"That seals it." Pause. "I have to go. Let's get together."

"Yes—I'll ask her to call you."

"Fine. We must not—by the way—hesitate to call the police."

* * *

Her friends told her to try to talk to her dad.

So, that evening after supper, he drank Bud and watched a cops and robbers sitcom. After it was over, she lowered the sound, and stood in front of him.

"Watcha doin'?" he asked.

"Daddy I gotta talk t'ya."

"Yeah? Whadda 'bout?" Pause. Snarl, sleepy-eyed, "I ain't got nuthin' t'say."

"Why ya sleepin' wit ya gun unduh ya pilla, huh?"

"Whya wanna know?"

"Cause I wanna."

"Watsit ya fuckin' business, huh? Ya fuckin' nosy—"

"Daddy, I gotta know! *Whya doin' it?*"

"Git outa m'way a new show's on."

Her eyes filled with tears as she stepped aside, saying:

"Daddy whyd'ya put th' crucifix on Ma's pilla? Ya scared 'er half t'death!"

His face turned a dull crimson, and the way he looked up at her, from under heavy lids, if looks could kill . . .

* * *

In the kitchen.

"Ma I tried t' talk wid 'im, I tried."

"Nah, it ain't no use." Pause. They looked at each other. "Dar," Ma said, "Whadda we gonna do?"

133

*　　*　　*

Next day, from a public phone at school.

"Doctuh Perry?"

"Yes Darlene. Are you okay?"

"Yeh. I tried t'talk t' 'im 'n he ain't—"

"Talking."

"Yeh." Pause. Her voice low. "He gimme a funny look."

A chill ran up Perry's spine: "What kind of funny look?"

"He kudda killed me." Pause. "Kin I see ya, Doctuh? Huh?"

"Yes. Hold on." Pause. "This afternoon at four?"

"Yeh. Okay."

"Thanks for calling."

She had difficulty understanding why he said that, but after an embarrassed silence—brief, she said goodbye. Leaned against the wall, dejected, as her friends stood around, looking evil, kinky, and dangerous, but they too were scared.

Went outside to the smoking area and lit up cigarettes.

"Whud he say?" A boy, with long, shaggy black hair and black leather jacket, jeans, boots.

"I see 'im at four."

They all went, at four, that afternoon, and waited outside in the parking lot, and smoked cigarettes while Darlene went inside the hospital, to see Doctor Perry.

*　　*　　*

The city where this took place, was rather small in population, but wide in area, so professional people tended to know each other, and several police officers knew Doctor Perry for he had treated them, as well as members of the family, and friends. Was a good man, in their esteem. Some officers also knew Roy Jones, and though indifferent if not defensive regarding psychiatry, in spite of his cool, rather distant presence, they thought he was okay, too. No one understood his lectures, at the Police Academy, on the psychology of the victim, that police officers must recognize victims as well as other people, went over their heads almost as fast as the concept of masochism.

Unable to stand it any longer, and almost in tears, Dar blurted out the fact of her father's gun under his pillow, and the crucifix— from off the wall above the bed—on her mother's pillow, and how it scared her and Ma so they didn't know what to do. Doctor Perry anxious, sad, and angry—

134

"Do you think I should call the police? I know them. They can be discreet."

No. Never.

"Dar, I'm a doctor, with a hospital full of patients. If your dad is doing these things — wait. Will you see Doctor Jones here? He's the psychiatrist. He can tell you what it means, and why your dad is doing it."

"Yeh?"

"Yes. I'll call him, and you can speak with him, and set up an appointment."

Her face dark, stolid, ignorant, an Indo-European rock, covered with moss.

But Doctor Jones was not in his office, for he was himself ill, with a cold, his recorded voice said, sounding like he had a cold. Bad one. A Doctor Henry would take all new patients. The voice of Jones gave Henry's telephone number.

Perry smiled.

Darlene at wits end with all this mystery.

"Jones is home with a bad cold," he said. "You are to phone this number, and say Dr. Jones recommended you. Give Dr. Henry my name and tell him to call me. I'll brief him for you."

She didn't know how far out he was going for her, and Ma.

And back to the wall, for something had to be done, to her own astonishment, she phoned Dr. Henry and set up an appointment, mentioning Dr. Perry, whom, to her surprise, Dr. Henry knew.

"Perry wants you to see me?" the voice said.

"Yeh." Pause. "Evvybuddy knows each utha, huh?"

"It's a small town in a small world, my dear. Would you tell me why you want to see me?"

There was something so nice, that seemed rather sweet, and warm, in his voice as he spoke of smallness, that disarmed her, and before she knew it, she told him. Her hair tickled. She thought of her friends, waiting for her. Dr. Henry asked,

"Did you ask him why?"

"YEH! YEH! I DID! But he wooden say nuthin' jus' looked at me, funny, like he kud kill me."

"Maybe you should phone the police?"

"Doctuh Perry said tuh." Pause. "I dunno." Pause. "Doctuh?"

"Yes?"

"Doctuh Perry sez you kin tell me why he's doin' these things, my Ma's scared outa her wits. Me too. 'N if I kin teller mebbe it'll help, ya know," she blushed. Began to pant.

"I know," he said. "Thursday, six?"

"Sooner. Is it gonna cost me?"

"Tomorrow evening at seven? We'll discuss that then."

"Seven? Yeh. Okay. Bye."

Dr. Henry telephoned Dr. Perry, who—after saying hello for they were professional friends—gave Dr. Henry all he knew on Darlene. Perry—

"It could be a police matter."

"I won't hesitate if it is."

But prayed it was not.

*   *   *

Her father knew something was going on. Her mother didn't say a word, and wore a mask over her everyday mask, so save the stitches in her lip and the dressing across the bridge of her nose, he saw nothing. He had seen very little anyway, and with her new mask she became a silhouette, and the walking shadow that represented her was a threat, thus in fear and confusion he remained closed, and silent.

The evening Dar went to her first session with Dr. Henry, her friends went with her, and waited outside, smoking cigarettes, in concerned wonderment after she had buzzed, declared who she was, and was buzzed inside. In she went. The door closed behind her. To her friends Darlene had crossed over, into *The Twilight Zone*.

On their fourth cigarette, a tall, slender, handsome blond man, neither young or old crossed the street, went up the steps of the same building, and repeated the same process as Darlene. Was admitted. After the door closed behind him, the kids outside looked at each other. In their modern mode of dress—boys with dyed long hair, jewelry and makeup, and the girls with short hair dyed wild colors, and bangles, rings, jewelry and faces made up, in leather and denim, all black, with black boots—their pale faces in swirls of smoke gave the scene an air of theater, as on stage in a theater of the street, among parked cars, in a city neighborhood, around 1100 A.D. during the Crusades, on the edge of the forest that stretched from one end of Europe to the other, a band of wounded, and disillusioned soldiers had gathered, and chosen this their site, for performances of morality plays, in which Death, his face pale white, dressed in a long black robe, played the leading role.

136

If

DR. HENRY lived in the Bohemian section of the city.

Besides being a therapist, his hobbies were walking, sitting on park benches and watching people, amateur boxing and the theater.

He had a most interesting group of patients.

For example, Dollie.

Dollie.

Tall, dark, and handsome.

Boyish, shy. Large-boned. Big feet.

Had graduated from an Eastern school, and through contacts — his drama teacher had had considerable experience — Dollie did miss getting the lead role in a big production, but was the understudy. It looked like a hit: a rather dark love story, with some comedy . . . but the actress who played the leading lady, in a way Dollie didn't understand, frightened him, and during rehearsals caused him such anxiety that her presence on the stage, as he sat in the wings, she stood so close to him on stage, in the last scene, he was almost ill, and in her farewell, almost within touching distance, he moved back, to have distance from her, otherwise he would vomit. The thought of having to play the lead man, to embrace her, and in passion to kiss her, confess his love — he prayed the leading man stay healthy. Two weeks before dress rehearsal the director told him in no uncertain terms, to see Dr. Henry, if he wanted the job. Said in confidence, of course, alone with Dollie, adding if Dollie had a problem interacting on stage with women, he'd best choose another profession. The Marines, for example. Being himself gay, the pointed look the director gave Dollie, hit home. That's how Dollie learned the first law of theater: the illusion rules supreme. As the curtain goes up, reality recedes into darkness, the stage blazes with light, and the play begins: reality trembles, distant and unreal: spellbound.

"Also," the director added: "You're good. I know you can do the part. I don't want to hurt your feelings, but our lead man, remember, is Mister Straight himself. He lives straight out on straight street, *he* takes *her,* for *granted*!" Pause. "Have I made myself clear?"

So the director telephoned Hen to tell him Dollie would be calling, and for Hen to set up a date for sessions to begin. But Dr. Hen interrupted saying he would look forward to hearing from Dollie, hoped the new play would be a hit, goodbye. The director, startled and a little hurt, remembered, yes, the idea was that the future patient must phone, not a friend or relative. "He thinks," mused the director aloud, "that I want to get in on the act." And if Hen had heard that, he would have said, "That's why you're the director." But there was more to that little game. Not a lot. A little. Good stuff, too.

Dollie did phone, in a fright. Hen asked him who had recommended him and Dollie mentioned the director. Good. They agreed on a date and an hour.

The first session began in a way that had it been a film or a play, the audience would have wept with laughter, for Dollie was the prototypical distraught and anxious fairy, his every feature deranged, perspiring, swishing, eyebrows up, blue eyes bugged, rubber-mouthed, wringing his hands, not knowing where to go Hen guided him to the couch Dollie agitated *zzz, zzzz* electric arranged himself like a folding ruler: flat out, face and toes up. Hen sat behind Dollie's head, pen and pad in hand.

"We'll discuss payments and schedules, but as my first interest is you," Hen said in a smiling voice, "what seems to be the problem?"

Funny little question.

Dollie began to answer but, he, he tried but, didn't know where or how, to begin.

"Things appear complex at first," Hen said.

"May I face you as I talk to you?" Dollie.

"Of course."

Done.

Sitting in an arm chair, facing Hen who sat beside a desk, Dollie more at ease, although having difficulty breathing, making theatrical gestures, rolling his eyes saying he hadn't done this . . . before, didn't know what . . . it was, my God . . .

"*I'm* not afraid of anything, *no* more than anyone else, I have *never* thought of myself as abnormal, or *neuro*tic, OH!" Rolling his eyes. "I had a happy childhood, and love my *parents*! and they love *me*, I don't know WHY it is that I'm HERE or so upSET," took a deep breath. Exhaled. Another. Exhaled. Inhaled, deep: "I'm the understudy for the leading man in a big production and I'm terrified of the leading LADY! I PRAY *NOTHING happens* to him," exhaling. Woebegone look at Hen, "If I have to go out there, on stage with her, I'll die . . . I mean it."

138

"Have you been in many plays?"

"Since college?"

Dollie didn't notice, but Hen switched tracks. "Yes," he said. Smiled.

"No."

"This is your first big chance?"

"Yes." Tears.

Hen passed over a box of tissues, which the patient used, rising and returning it to desk top, placing used ones in a glass ashtray, returned to his chair, and sat down. Drained, but alert and clear-eyed.

"I see," Hen said. "I've heard of this production of your play —" Hen smiled —". . . why are you afraid of her?"

But Dollie was impressed with the "your play" strategy, and thought, *it could be my play. It could be! It might very well be MY play!* His blood warmed, a feel of cool power ran through, in a wink of hope something might happen to the leading man, Dollie blinked, leaned forward, and said, with a sleepy-eyed sneer and snarl, nasty, meaning to hurt,

"When I was a boy I thought I was straight, but baby, once I crossed over, good-bye pussy! I haven't had a hand on anything but men, since," widening his eyes as if insulted, twisting his lips in a sneer, but in sudden change his face cleared, eyes grew solemn, mouth composed, looked right at Hen, and cocked an eyebrow, and with a ghost of a smile, said —

"If I was straight, I'd make a play for her."

"If?" Hen asked, hearing the word "play."

Dollie sulky, nasty, "But I'm not straight, Doc-*tor*. Don't lay that shit on *me*!"

"You say you're an actor?"

A veil crossed Dollie's face. He didn't answer. Hen didn't move, but sat there, eyes on him. Dollie uneasy, just a little alarmed. "What do you mean?"

"Didn't you say you're an actor?"

Again Dollie silent, but at length sighed, as in okay, you win, "Yes."

"If you were straight, you'd make a play for her?"

"Just what I said, although I don't know why," in sing song, "in fact I can't imagine!"

"But you want that part — you're the understudy?"

Pause. "Yes. What are you *doing?*"

"Don't you see what you've said?"

Confusion. "Yes, and no?" Glanced at the box of tissues.

Hen leaned forward, the room seemed filled with light, yet

139

in an odd way like a cave, sunlight streaming in—

"Let's change it around like this," Hen said, "If you were an actor, you'd make a play for her that you could act in." Sitting back with a subtle, rather arch look. Dollie gaped.

"Do you mean, do you MEAN I should *act* straight, and chase AFTER *her*?"

Hen didn't answer. Look baffled, meaning he was thinking. And just as he was about to say "not quite" he changed his mind—but Dollie stood up, with a rather mad smile, and pointing at Hen, said,

"No. You mean I should act straight for the part in the play!" He threw his arms in the air and stretched, a long complete stretch, motions exaggerated in a sexual way, showing Hen his body, before he sat down, and said, "Why didn't *I* think of that?" Pause. "To act straight." He swished in his chair a little, then composed himself, inhaled, and in a voice a shade deeper, his face calm, he said, "I can do it." Pause. But the thought of *her* broke him down, lips trembling, perspiration . . . "Not with *her*." Whimpered.

"What is that line about 'to *act it* is to *be it*'? Isn't Olivier every part he plays?"

"Yes," Dollie murmured, eyes glazed. "To act straight is to be straight."

Hen smiled. "For your moment on the stage."

Dollie sighed, lowered his head, nodding agreement.

"If I . . . want that part."

Hen's face was warm, his eyes kind.

"But *how*?" Dollie whispered, looking up, leaning forward, "*How*? I have women friends but I wouldn't, I couldn't get IT UP DOC*TOR*! I wouldn't DREAM of sex, with them," he shuddered, in revulsion. "*Impossible*!"

Hen looked just a little like a wolf. "Dream?" he said. "If you were straight, you'd make a play for her, but not being straight, wouldn't dream of sex. Very interesting. If, and dream. Possibility and fantasy. Put them together, look what you have."

"You're not talking to me," Dollie said, angry. "You're talking to yourself, and I don't know what you mean!"

Hen held up a fist. "We have a rock hard reality. Be straight for your play, for you in your play, for her in your play—be as straight a guy under those lights as there is: turn yourself inside out, straight up: first you: stage one: be a *man*. Stage two: she's yours."

Dollie laughed.

"Be a *man*!" Puffed out his chest, raised his shoulders and clasped hands before his chest, bulging his muscles, surprised to see how strong he was, he stood up, all butch. Parading around the room. "I'm a

140

man." Squared off like a prizefighter, jabbed left, right, into air, laughed: " 'Cha-lee, I coulda been a contenda!' "

"Keep an eye on straight men. They're a little different from us," Hen confided. "And take her out, talk with her, get to know her."

"She has a boyfriend."

"She has the lead in a play that's looking big. He'll expect it."

"Shall I tell her about — you?"

Hen shrugged, smiled. Big smile. Old buddy. "Why me? Why not you? It's your play."

At the door to the room — Hen's Den it was called — Dollie turned, raised left arm and fist — cried,

"*MAN* POWER!"

Exit.

While watching *The MacNeil/Lehrer News Hour* that evening, Dexter, Hen's lover, said,

"Don't bully that young actor."

His voice was gruff, in warmth. He was a shaggy man, wore tweed, smoked a briar pipe.

"Did you think I was?" Hen asked.

"The tone of your voice was leading up to it." Pause. "I didn't say you did, I'm saying don't."

Hen kissed Dexter's hand: "Okay, I won't."

Dexter was an amateur landscape photographer, and as his darkroom was next to Hen's Den, and the wall was thick, and sound-proofed on Hen's side, Dexter heard muffled voices, but knowing Hen's, could judge what was said by the tone.

Nothing new in Dexter saying that, advice well taken.

Director delighted.

"Excellent!"

Dollie happy and proud, determined, began to warm to the leading lady, in deference, during rehearsals, until a casual dialogue had been established and he asked her out for a drink, okay, and seated at a table at a sidewalk cafe, with a glass of chilled white wine, he said he had begun therapy, that he had never done it before, and at first was very nervous.

"What was the problem?" she asked, with that knowing smile that said she knew.

"You," Dollie blushed. And told her why.

At first she thought it was funny. "Terrified of *me*?" she mused.

141

"Who ever could be? And why? I'm such a . . . pushover," she murmured. "It isn't me."

"Well I don't know who else it is," he laughed, "but I don't want to be, I mean afraid of you," in a tone of apology. "If Harry gets sick, or something . . . I've got to be in love with you."

"Sure, that's right. Good. Good for you. I like you," she said, and he saw she meant it. "You might be a little too sensitive, but we all gotta have something wrong." She sipped wine, looking at him. "You're good looking, Dollie, you're bright and you've got a nice body, and I don't know if anyone has ever told you, but you're stronger than you think."

He hailed a cab for her, and held the door. Before she got in, she said,

"If I can help, let me know. If you want to talk about it, do. Don't keep it back." Her eyes were level. "Bye."

As the cab pulled out into traffic, he found himself standing on the sidewalk, watching it, thinking he wouldn't tell George, his roommate, who was becoming each day more hostile to Dollie's play, and Dollie's problem.

Dollie mentioned this to Hen, during the next session, after the news that he and the leading lady had become friends. She was supportive. Things were looking up.

The dress rehearsal a success, so too opening night, and good reviews, a week later still sold out, booked in fact, until Thanksgiving, so the session with Hen that preceded opening night, Dollie thought would be his last, why should there be any more? Of course Hen agreed, in his radical theory of low-cost, rapid therapy, getting patients back on the street, out in the world to function again, to return if desired for deep therapy.

Dollie had given Hen two tickets, Hen very excited, Dexter too, they couldn't *wait* to see it!

"Keep in touch with me regarding George," Hen said, at the door, to which Dollie, relieved, said of course, yet as Hen reached for the doorknob, he paused.

"After the play has finished its run," Hen said, his voice, and facial expressions quite different from the excited theater-goer, "call me, so we may schedule a session."

"A session?"

"Yes, would you call?"

Hen the eager audience, Dollie blinked.

"Sure," he said, laughing at he knew not what, as Hen, too, laughed, opening the door.

142

Hen and Dexter indeed eager to see the play, in case something happened to Harry, they'd know the part Dollie would play.

And as sure as snow in Siberia, just before the third Saturday matinee in the fourth month of the production, Harry, the leading man, fractured his left ankle and knee in an auto collision outside the theater, and while being taken to the hospital in an ambulance, Dollie walked out on stage, ready, before a full house, to face the leading lady, kneel at her feet, look up at her, and confess, in tears, his love.

Members of the audience who had seen it before, along with the crew, stagehands, prompter, stand-ins, agreed that the leading lady gave her part new zest, and the play in all, as if awakened from being good, became a sensation. The emotional, dramatic and sex scenes were scalding, and the final scene as she leaves him, and he, in a rage, tells her to go, and in hysterics she does, leaving him alone at center stage, face in his hands . . . to the music, their song: *The Nearness of You,* to the curtain, in slow descent.

Dollie, after the performance, of course, phoned Hen to tell him the great news. Hen overjoyed. Dollie mailed him two tickets, not easy to get, so later, the following week, after that performance, backstage, Hen ecstatic, gave Dollie a bouquet of roses. Dollie blushed. And the director, seeing Hen, was elated. So too the leading lady, meeting Dr. Henry, Dollie's miracle-working shrink, all round, a happy, festive evening, affectionate, as a wonderful reunion, and before Hen and Dexter left, Hen took Dollie aside, and with a little cackle, reminded Dollie to be sure and telephone, for an appointment, after the show closed. Somewhat baffled, but dazed and cheered, Dollie agreed.

Hen hugged him.

"Don't forget!"

George, Dollie's roommate, moved out. Having been cynical about that Dr. Hen business, and as the play went on, Dollie acting as straight as train tracks, after quite a long affair, it was over. AIDS or no AIDS. Rather seek a new partner than live with someone who had become famous overnight because of acting straight in a play, a role George despised him for playing, although he wouldn't say so, his tone of voice, veiled contempt and jokes, revealed his hatred of women.

"Men who hate women hate themselves," Dr. Hen said, on the phone. "And we can do without that. With your career ahead of you, you can afford to select someone who understands you."

"That's true," Dollie said. "But except for that one thing, we got along fine. Of course, he hated you, too."

"And himself, as well, which as his hatred turned on you, he had to leave, because he couldn't tolerate hating himself hating you. That was a little too much." Pause. "How are you otherwise?"

"Fine, and I have made new friends . . . am being very careful, too. Safe sex only."

"Good. Don't hesitate to call, and don't forget, after the show —"

"I know!" Dollie cried. "I haven't forgotten!" although angry, he laughed, hearing Hen clucking.

Not long after, after a party Dollie gave, the leading lady spent the night with him, and using condoms, he had sex with her, before they went to sleep, and on awakening. Breakfast together. Went to a movie that afternoon, before the evening performance, and a few days later, they did it again, and he realized he and his leading lady had something going. Phoned Hen and told him. Hen said maybe he was a closet bi-sexual, how's the play going, hm?

So, late the following year, after the last performance, everyone chipped in for a party that people discussed long into the future: *everybody* showed up, it had gone on all night, well into the following day, the ex-leading man and his ex-leading lady had their last fling in a tender, and memorable farewell. Have remained friends ever since. She of course is married, and in another big production. Dollie is somewhere in Europe, starring in another film. He had played the lead in the movie version of the play . . .

So the two leading stars had hugged each other tight, couldn't believe it was over, how sad it always will be, after that last curtain comes down!

Dollie telephoned Hen, and a session was arranged. Dollie somewhat irritated, figuring Hen wanted to wrap it up, congratulate him, give him a hug, wish him well in Hollywood — for Dollie's agent had broken the news — and in Hen's professional way, as a gentleman, would urge Dollie to keep in touch, if Dollie ever needed help, don't hesitate to call.

But as Dollie sat in that chair, it felt odd, and Hen looked rather different, sitting in his chair, beside his desk. The ashtray was there, so too the box of tissues. Hen looked pale, in fact a little luminous, his yellow banded black eyes had a tiny glow, and raising his chin a notch, leaned forward, eyes expanding —

"The play is over. Who is she?"

"Joan Hoffman, lives on Green Street, near —"

"The play is over!" Hen hissed. *"Who is she!"*

"I — don't know what you mean." Dollie taken aback. Hen's face darkened, a vein in his forehead stood out, as he growled.

"None of that! Didn't you ever *dream*?"

"I-I don't know. I don't remember!"

A soft tapping on the wall. Hen sat back with a smile, as Dollie turned, to look. Hen, sleepy-eyed.

"I'm having some electrical work done."

"Oh."

Controlling his temper, keeping his voice reasonable, Hen said,

"You said she terrified you. She made you throw up. You cringed from her. Who was she, who had that effect on you? Who would cause you such agony? Joan Hoffman? No. Who, then? The play is over, Dollie. All masks come down."

"I understand and I—do not. I had no idea . . . I never thought. . ." frowning, thinking.

"If you don't find out, you'll remain a homosexual playing games with being straight. Do you want to do that?"

Dollie frightened, paled. "No. God, no."

"Good. We must be what we are." Pause. "Let's find out who she is. What do you say?" Hen paused, letting it sink in. "Only you can tell me, only you can let us know." Pause. "On the other hand you can stand up, and fly out to Beverly Hills and never know, forever."

"But, you said if I acted straight in the play I was cured! How straight could I act—or be! I had a long, terrific affair with her!"

Hen laughed: "Who is cured? No! My gambit was I wanted to know who it was who had such an impact on you, and if you acted straight in the play, you'd find out."

"You mean *you'd* find out!"

"If I know, you know." Pause. "So, we don't know." Pause. "Let's find out."

"Is it important?"

"Yes. Very."

"Can I do it before I leave?"

"If we work hard."

"Okay. Let's find out."

"Splendid," Hen beamed, and taking pen and pad in hand, gestured, please,

"Lie down."

In his element Hen had that long look so difficult to understand, in a love of peering through layers of veils . . . to listen, and as the mystery cleared in the first act, it was a razzle-dazzle thriller, a classic for the audience of two as the two players searched, entering to the surprise of one, in the plan of the other, the second act: who was the man in *Man*-power? Who was the man in, "Be a man." Was there an image? A dream? Before the grand third act, the climax of the self responding to the previous two. For Hen had tricked his patient, for he could be devious. He knew, for example, that the play was never over. Never. In the cold fact of death, memories lived on, and as patients who walked out, after the final session, were so often certain to return, in person, or through a phone call, a letter, or a recommendation, and this aspect of his discipline gave him courage to continue, as long as he too, was on stage.

"Tell me where you were born," Hen began. "Your earliest memories. Geographical locations, proper names and descriptions as close, as accurate to your memory as possible. The same goes for dreams. Okay." Pause. "Begin."

"Do you want me to talk about my mother?"

Silence. Dollie wished he could see out of the top of his head, to see Dr. Henry's face, but no. He gazed at the ceiling.

"I miss my father," he said. "Always have."

Silence.

Dollie sighed, stretched his legs, crossed his feet, and cleared his throat. "Do you want me to—free associate?"

"Not today."

Dollie yawned, and for which he couldn't account, he felt sleepy. Yawned again. Big one . . . he sighed.

As the front door of a house is closed by an unseen hand, and the back door opened by another, as his lids came down he recalled where he was, his mind as clear as an empty glass, gave his full name, the place of his birth, its geographical location, and the date. He told his mother's maiden name, in a flash to his father's brother Gene, who had fascinated him, and Dr. Hen heard, in the tone of Dollie's voice, a sudden realization of his mother. Dollie saw her face before him—he'd seen her with Gene, standing and talking, or having coffee in the kitchen, there was a way she looked at Gene, who was married to Aunt Dabney, they had four kids—Dollie sat up, turned, and looked at Dr. Hen.

"I forgot!" Eyes wide. Dollie stared at Hen. "Gene, my uncle, had been an actor! But gave it up to go into business, get married and have a family. I saw his scrapbook! He was *good*! Got great reviews. Played the fool in *Lear,* the role of Lucky in *Godot* before the world knew who Beckett was! and—" hand across his brow, eyes closed, "his wife was my Aunt Dabney who didn't like her name and changed it to Dollie! She from whom I took my nickname! because—is it because she was married to Gene? And because my mother—?"

Hen, as still as a statue, head raised in a trance, his eyes so wide they captured the top half of his narrow face, and below his curved, and narrow nose, his small, pale lips were parted as he breathed, over

146

tips of crooked teeth, he, as neat as a pin in a gray and white three piece suit, white shirt, dark blue tie. Black leather shoes, pointed tips, mirror shine, his eyes seeing beyond the room out onto a vast white plane, and on Dollie's mention of his mother's maiden name, two lines, one silver the other pink, were flung against white, where they froze, and on the mention of father a great wave of red slashed out above the other lines, and red dripped down, on them, to freeze. Uncle Gene a grand wash of green, in part covered the red, and Aunt Dabney — Aunty Dollie turned into a pale blue loop, and so it went, with every name and image of recall, the lines on the white plane intensified, and soon, so soon, right away, almost at once it became a work of art.

"And because of your mother — ?"

Hen's question was warm, and encouraging, and Dollie began to talk, again, while Hen watched the painting change before his eyes, and took notes on his pad, or, you could say, more or less copied what he was seeing, using words and symbols in a personal shorthand, in a hopeful imitation of the original. But yet the same, yes of course. Mother loving the actor, the man, the power, lines flung into view as Dollie talked: wasn't language line and color, in that room? Yes. And vivid! Clear as rain in the green jungle, as a yellow moon over a bluegray mountain, and a painted face on an empty stage, singing a song.

The White

THE DENTIST had told his patient that the last, upper right section that had to be done, was going to be bad. He said the word — "bad" — with a look of concern, so the patient, knowing what the look, word (and tone of voice) implied, was prepared as best he could as he sat in the chair.

The patient was a middle-aged man who had for fifteen years seen an older dentist who had not kept up with recent advances in D.D.S. work, and forbade his patients to brush with toothpaste mixed with baking soda, and rinse with hydrogen peroxide.

The man had lost a cap on his right front tooth, which had been replaced by a temporary that a few weeks later, while he was eating corn on the cob, fell off. His dentist was on vacation, so the patient found another dentist, a young man new in the neighborhood, who affixed the temporary back into place, and said,

"I should warn you that your gums are in very bad shape, like here." Reached in. Took hold of some teeth. They waggled. "If you don't have periodontal work done soon, well, you're going to be in trouble." Gave his patient a pointed look. "You do not want false teeth."

"No, no," murmured the other, embarrassed. "I don't." Pause. "What should I do?"

"Brush your teeth with toothpaste mixed with baking soda. Rinse with hydrogen peroxide. After every meal. Once a day brush for three minutes, and concentrate on it."

"If I do, will it help reduce the periodontal stuff?"

"No. Look."

The dentist, showing sensitivity, was gentle, but his patient felt the needle-thin probe go deep, into the gums around his teeth.

"See?" Holding it, fingertip showing, as on an oil gauge, the depth of rotten gum.

So the patient had little to do but get busy on it, and borrowed enough money to get the lower and upper left done. The lower left went pretty well. A lot of blood with nasty looking (and awful tasting) black chunks spat from between lips, half his mouth numbed by Novocain, so it dribbled down his chin (from that visit on he wore a red sweatshirt). Yet the work seemed to go pretty fast,

149

and sooner than expected the dentist was sewing up, and of course it didn't hurt, and the patient found himself interested in what was going on: the first session was in a sense an introduction, rather a learning experience.

The dentist had packed into the spaces he had opened up, and sewn closed, what looked like a pale pink gum, which on instructions the patient was to take great care not to let get loose. Don't brush. Appointment made for two weeks later.

Two weeks later stitches removed, teeth and gums looked good, the patient a little shocked by how much gum the dentist — the periodontist — had cut away, and mentioned it, to which the doctor (at that point — dental surgeon) said there had been a *lot* of gum decay.

So, going easy at first and following instructions, the patient brushed, and soon the lower left looked and felt great. The dentist/surgeon decided to do the upper left next, and agreed that because of a bridge on the lower front, and two capped front teeth, lower and upper front wouldn't be operated on (although later he did, by combining it with the work on upper left and upper right). He would then do the lower right, and last, upper right.

On the upper left, the patient learned what serious periodontal surgery was.

The doc had said that was "bad" too, showing his patient how deep the probe went, but because of the relative ease with which the lower left had been cared for, the patient didn't know what "bad" was, and as he had had problems with his teeth all his life, "bad" was relative, maybe a word that was meant as a warning: as things would get going, what would result would be "bad." But from the doctor's point of view, it was bad *bad,* and though he was too much a non-verbal person to think this poor guy doesn't know what's going to hit him, experience had taught him to prepare himself for his patient's ordeal. He hadn't wanted to be a dentist because he couldn't be a doctor, he wanted to be a dentist, and practice periodontal work because it interested him, and he liked it, and, besides, he liked people. Nothing made him happier than to inform a patient to return twice a year for a checkup, or when doc went to the bank, and deposited the check. A job well done, everyone happy all round, even his wife, with whom he discussed his patients.

However, the doctor was a little put off by this patient, this middle-aged guy with the "bad" gums, because the older guy was verbal and knew it, so no doubt to give doc a little in return, as the surgery progressed (and the preparation for bridgework began: filing down of teeth, making a little ridge around each tooth, up under the gum), the patient, a buyer and salesman in the toy department in the local department store, was used to talking to people — wholesale people, and retail customers, he had an answer for everything, was a good judge of character, therefore knew what questions to ask, and how to ask them, so his

"What's that?"

caused the dentist to pause, and think before he answered (*patient positive!*: doc wasn't used to listening because his wife did the talking, was possible his mom had, too). So he didn't like to listen?

"Why did you do that?"

Or:

"What are you about to do?"

Thus began, or perhaps intensified — on doc's part — the classical practice of the dentist asking the patient a question, with the patient unable to answer, mouth full of cotton, spit remover looped over lower lip, part paralyzed by Novocain. Dentist chuckles, patient growls, mumbles, *agisff — ingoummminllya* ("Take this stuff out of my mouth and I'll tell you"). Ha ha, smiles the dentist (to himself), so, in this case the patient, realizing his impact on the doctor, decided to let enough alone, unless of course something caught his curiosity to a degree he couldn't help asking . . .

The scraping and cutting process began in the rear of the mouth, and moved forward, and in the work on his upper left, the doctor's nurse came in and helped swab blood, with the small, 2″ square gauze pads, for as he had said, the area was "bad." He spat out and rinsed a horrible amount of plaque, blood, bloodclots, decay, at one point tilted back in the chair, the back of his mouth had filled with blood.

"Rinse."

He sat forward as the chair lifted, and straightened. He spat and rinsed. Rinsed again. Again. Fingertips — cheeks, chin, upper lip — smeared with blood, so too the paper bib, and, perhaps his red sweatshirt. He glanced at the doctor, who had a complicated expression. Eyes wide in knowledge of his hurting, but dark in determination. The patient followed the chair as it tilted back.

The doctor had, patient recalled, lanced two areas (and he would do that again, on the right side) (lower), so that during surgery, they wouldn't hemorrhage, but midway on the upper left, the bleeding became very heavy, almost four hands stopping it, doctor daubing, saturated in a wink, placed a pile of pads on his patient's bibbed chest, which became his work area, splattered with blood. Scraped, hard, deep up under the gums.

"Rinse."

151

Done.

Again.

Patient aware the doc was determined, nothing would stop him, scrape and scrape more, harder, using fingers, not arm: an arm stroke, in a slip, would go through a cheek, deep into a jaw, or roof of mouth.

"Rinse."

Done.

Around the eyetooth the patient's head, as if shot, sprang away from the doctor's hands, doctor seeing the patient's forehead beaded with sweat: the Novocain was wearing off. Diseased pockets in gums above each tooth so filled with rot, the nerves were blocked with matter like black slime, into which the doctor shot another jolt, of Novocain, placed the needle on his patient's bib, and went back to work, listening to his patient groan. Nurse wiped patient's forehead.

"I know," doc said.

Patient's eyes opened, closed.

Doc went on to the end, prepared sewing needle and sutures, and completed the task. Same instructions. Two weeks. Patient walked out of the office shaken, as doc and his nurse cleaned up.

For the next round, the lower right, the patient had learned a little about periodontal surgery, had learned there were no other alternatives but sit and take it, or fling everything away, leap free from the chair, spit all the cotton and stuff from the mouth, scream a demand for false teeth, and ripping paper bib off, rush to the nearest bar.

But short of that there was a rather vague, and not unpleasant relationship between the good patient and the good dentist. The lower right went okay, save heavy bleeding. And two weeks later doc said, regarding the last—upper right, that the rear tooth (a molar), and the gum around it was "bad."

" 'Bad,' " patient said.

The doctor nodded. "Bad."

"Worse than—" tapped his upper left.

Doc nodded. "Worse than that."

This meant it was almost certain that the Novocain would wear off before doc was finished, and that the work would proceed no matter. So it was.

So it did. But.

They both got a surprise.

Patient's face felt like a cow's hoof, so as doc began in the back, on the rear molar, patient felt nothing, yet glancing at him, saw doc had a frown, and made a sign he wanted to rinse. The chair rose, patient rinsed, again, and asked,

"What's the matter?"

152

"There's decay on that molar that didn't show up on the X-rays."
Pause. "It's bad."

The patient was lowered in the chair and the doctor returned
to his labor. He worked on that tooth from every angle, he used the
drill with a couple of different drill bits. He scraped, and drilled,
sanded, scraped, deep up into the gum: lots of blood, and rot, and
the word,

"Rinse,"

was obeyed.

The front of the patient's upper lip, near his eyetooth, began to
tingle, his body went tense, hands and fingers gripped the chair, doc
was using his chest again as a worktable, and bloody instruments,
and pads were strewn, including a loaded hypodermic. The doctor
threw away each needle after use. They were thread-thin, and bent.
At the end of that day—of the whole day—bent needles on the patient's chest, pads—a battlefield, as doc had worked forward, not able
to wait for the drug to take for the certain loss of previous injections,
already wearing off, he worked his way forward, nurse at hand, for
the patient it was the worst ever. Afterward, hands, fingers and mouth
twitching out of control, the patient sat up in the chair as doc and
nurse cleaned up a real bloody mess. The patient's hair stuck up on
the back of his head, lower faced streaked and speckled, but his eyes
were bright, and he raised his right hand, finger up—

"That rear molar, you scraped until it was white, didn't you?"

"Sure," after a brief pause. "So?"

"I saw it!"

"You *saw* it!" Jaw dropped.

The middle-aged buyer and toy salesman laughed, a grotesque
sight, as the doctor/dentist stood, astonished.

Three weeks later. At her apartment. By candlelight.

"What do you think it was?" she asked, over shrimp and white
wine. "Did you hypnotize yourself?"

"I don't know. I realized the pain was going to be so—intense.
My lip had begun to tingle, meaning the Novocain was wearing off.
He knew, too, but he kept scraping away at that rear molar. You
know me, and details, I began to wonder where he was on that molar,
and though I couldn't tell, I kind of drifted, and sank into the numb-
ness, yet certain of coming pain, feeling the pressure of him scraping, watching in the little round mirror, wiping blood off it—"

Holding fork poised, she said, "This is disgusting, don't stop!"

"He kept on, and the stuff he was scraping off was black, I saw
it in the mirror, I saw a spot of white appear, which as he scraped

grew larger, and realized his task was to make the whole tooth—"

"White."

"Yes. Don't interrupt me. And he said, before I left," squeezing lemon over shrimp, "that all my teeth are white." Had a bite. "And I realized that his job is to make teeth white."

"Make teeth white."

"Yes." Pause. "Just part of the periodontal process."

But she was so amused she didn't hear him, she was amused clear through, and she said, "So you told him you *saw* it, that you saw the white. Ha ha ha! Not only did you *see* it, you told him you did! He must have thought you mad!"

She couldn't stop laughing, as she reached for her glass, her bushy red curls shaking, freckled face lined with laughter, she raised her head. Dark blue eyes glared down at him, hand raising the glass, her teeth were large, and long, and her lips were scarlet.

"That's wicked, George. *Wicked!*"

1981–1987
New York

154

Printed June 1988 in Santa Barbara & Ann Arbor
for the Black Sparrow Press by Graham Mackintosh
& Edwards Brothers, Inc. Design by Barbara Martin.
This edition is printed in paper wrappers; there
are 250 cloth trade copies; 150 hardcover copies
have been numbered & signed by the author; & 26
lettered copies are handbound in boards by Earle
Gray each signed & with an original drawing by
Fielding Dawson.

Photo: Gerard Malanga

Fielding Dawson was born in New York in 1930. He grew up in Kirkwood, Missouri, attended Black Mountain College from 1949 until 1953, and after two years in the Army, moved to New York where he yet lives. Aside from his writing he is an exhibiting artist. He also has taught in prisons, and is completing a novel, *The House of D.*, which concerns that experience.